DARK IS HER NATURE

SCHOOL OF NECESSARY MAGIC™ BOOK ONE

JUDITH BERENS   MARTHA CARR   MICHAEL ANDERLE

DARK IS HER NATURE TEAM

Thanks to the JIT Readers

James Caplan
Kelly O'Donnell
John Ashmore
Micky Cocker
Peter Manis
John Raisor
Larry Omans

If we've missed anyone, please let us know!

Editor
Lynne Stiegler

From Martha

To everyone who still believes in magic
and all the possibilities that holds.
To all the readers who make this
entire ride so much fun.
And to my son, Louie and the wonderful Katie
who remind me all the time of what
really matters and how wonderful
life can be in any given moment.

From Michael

To Family, Friends and
Those Who Love
To Read.
May We All Enjoy Grace
To Live The Life We Are
Called.

The sparking red fireball lit up the dank alley, making shadows bounce off the stone walls. The heat and malevolent aura of the dark wizards saturated the air around Izzie and her parents. They hadn't seen the attack coming, not at all. They were walking home after seeing a movie during the last bit of Izzie's summer vacation before she started high school. Her mother pushed Izzie behind her as she deflected the fireball. She fired a return shot and knocked one of the wizards off his feet.

"Not here," her father growled, his long silver hair blowing back from the force of magic. "We don't want trouble."

The dark wizard cackled from the shadows. "Trouble? Too late."

The fight began in earnest and clouds of smoke rose from the crushed stone along the walls, and the smoldering ashes of the magical fireballs. Izzie brought her hand to her mouth to cover the stench, then determinedly put her hands out in front of her. If there was going to be a fight, Izzie wouldn't back down just because she was a teenager. Her chest warmed as she pulled the light to her. The magic rolled from her fingertips into her palms and she swirled it around, collecting more and more energy.

"Find your target," she whispered before jumping out from behind her mom.

She threw the fireball as hard as she could as it struck one of the wizards in the chest. The man flew backward and crashed into a wall. Pieces crumbled down from above, covering him in dust as he groaned, his shirt smoldering and smoking.

"Good hit, Izzie." Her dad looked back at her as a stream of light clashed with the oncoming blows.

"No! She could be killed," her mother cried desperately.

"She knows how to fight for her life, just like the rest of us." He gave her a comforting look and reached out for her hand.

Her mother nodded, then pulled her long dark hair behind her and secured it at the nape of her neck. The three stood facing the onslaught as the dark wizards shot magic from their wands. Izzie stood between her parents, her shining arms stretched out in front of her and her beams of light mixed with theirs. The light and dark streams collided and rained down, but suddenly the attack stopped. Izzie lowered her hands and squinted down the dark alley.

A tall man, his hood pulled low to shadow his face, cackled loudly as he stepped forward. Izzie's father sent a fireball toward him, but the man swished it away with his wand and ignored the explosion behind him. He moved slowly forward, deflecting every attempt they made. He and the other wizards raised their wands, sending dark streams down the alley. Izzie and her parents dove to the side, rolled across the ground, and pressed their backs against the walls.

The wizards cast a torrent of fire that crashed over their heads, barely missing them. Izzie tucked her head as her father stared at her mother. He nodded and the three of them stood up, dodging dark magic by mere inches. Izzie remembered what she had been taught, brought the energy into her stomach and forced it through her hands. Bolts of white light whizzed past the wizards, catching their cloaks and sending white flames up their backs. Izzie's mother followed up with a spray of sparks, causing some of the wizards to scream as they ripped their cloaks from their backs.

The head of the group shouted and threw one large orb down the alley, but Izzie and her parents stood ready to deflect. As it hit the center, it burst into hundreds of smaller orbs. Izzie slowly backed up in alarm as the dark magic plowed toward them. Her parents stepped forward and lifted their hands, their light shifting in front of them and spreading out like a translucent wall. As the orbs hit the light wall they burst as sparks sizzled to the ground. Izzie looked at her father, whose hands shook. He had blood trickling down his arm from his shoulder. One of the orbs had broken through and hit him, but he held firm.

"They are tiring," her father called, "but this will only hold them for a moment. Be ready to run."

The light made by her parents glowed brighter and the wall turned into a thick fog and blew toward the wizards, knocking them back. The fog hid them for the moment, but it was already starting to dissipate. Izzie's parents grabbed her hands and rushed her out to the sidewalk. The people walking past looked at them strangely since her father was grasping onto a bloody shoulder.

"Move fast," her mother whispered.

They moved at almost a jog, taking corners quickly and passing through different alleys to try to throw the wizards off their trail. When they reached the house, her mother sent an orb through the window to check for someone who might be inside waiting for them. When it returned clean they rushed inside.

Her father pulled off his torn t-shirt and her mother began to heal him, the magic brightening the room. Izzie's father grimaced.

Her mother turned her head. "Izzie, go to your room, get your duffel bag, and pack as much as you can carry. We don't know how long we have. We have to hurry. They will be coming for us." Her mother turned back, finishing the spell on her father's shoulder.

Izzie nodded and bolted up the stairway and into her room. She flipped on the desk light and paused, staring at her room, the place she had spent almost all her time. It hit her then that she was leaving, and without all of her things. She shook her head and raced to the closet, pulling out the duffel and opening it on her bed. She shoved her clothes inside, then grabbed a couple of her favorite books and squeezed them on top. She sighed as she looked back from her doorway. She didn't understand, but she knew that if her parents wanted to leave it was serious.

She switched off the light and headed back downstairs,

where her mother and father waited. Her mother handed her a long black cloak. They had bags as well, and her mother had tears in her eyes, but was trying to hold back for Izzie's sake. Her father went to her mother and pressed his forehead against hers, closing his eyes.

"It will be okay, but we *have* to go," he whispered. She nodded and looked at Izzie, then grasped her daughter's hand tightly.

The three walked swiftly down the street to where the car was parked, searching for any signs of the wizards. Izzie had never seen her parents so frightened, but she knew it would be okay because they were together. When they reached their SUV, Izzie threw her bag in the back and climbed in and her mother and father took the front seats.

They headed down the road and took the ramp for the highway, her mother finally pulling her hood down. She looked at Izzie's father and grabbed his hand, and he looked at her and sighed.

"We have to hide her." Izzie's father sounded panicked.

"I know," her mother replied. "But where? These wizards won't stop, not until they know it's taken care of. We might do better if we stick together."

"You know that's not true." He squeezed her mother's hand tighter.

"What are you guys talking about?" Izzie asked frowning.

"Just sit back and relax," her father advised, looking into the rearview mirror.

"No!" Izzie shouted. "You are talking about me; about taking me somewhere and leaving me. I won't do it."

Izzie shook her head and tears formed in her eyes. Her mother let go of her father's hand and sighed, then nodded at him. He pulled off the highway and stopped, and her mother got out and climbed into the back with Izzie. She took both of her daughter's hands in hers and looked at her comfortingly.

"Sweetie, we will *always* make the best choices for you."

Izzie shook her head. "Being with you *is* the best choice. I'll go wherever you're going and fight with you. Don't leave me behind!"

"Izzie!" Her mother snapped, then grabbed her shoulders and softened her tone. "You have to go somewhere safe, somewhere you can be protected. We can't do that for you, not in the best way. This will be the best thing for you."

"You don't want me to slow you down." Izzie's tears were a flood now.

"That's not it at all. We want you to be safe, even if it means we aren't together for a while. We will see each other again, I promise. Come here."

Her mother pulled her into a hug and looked at her father. He let out a deep breath and started to drive again, putting as much distance between them and the wizards as he could. Izzie laid her head on her mother's shoulder, and looked out into the darkness. Everything was happening so fast, and she didn't understand most of it. She didn't want to be away from her parents. They were her best friends; the three amigos. They were the only people she ever felt safe with.

Izzie knew her mother believed they would get back together, but the wrenching feeling in Izzie's gut made her think otherwise. She wasn't ready to say goodbye to them and go out on her own, but she feared she wasn't going to be given a choice. Things weren't at all how Izzie had thought they would be, but she could only follow her parents' instructions and hope for the best.

2

The SUV turned down a dirt road and Izzie could see fireflies in the distance shimmering over the fields. Her father slowed down as they approached a wide iron gate with the Oriceran crest on the top. The headlights reflected against the metal, bringing a tall dark-haired woman into view. As he turned the car off and Izzie's mother looked at her with a gentle smile.

"Come on, we're here," she whispered.

Izzie climbed out and looked at the gates. She recognized them from the pictures her father had shown her of the School of Necessary Magic. The school year hadn't begun yet, and the grounds were dark and quiet with only the sounds of crickets in the air. The woman stepped through the gates and waved her wand, sending an orb of light down the path they had just driven up.

"Izzie, this is Ms. Grant. She teaches here at your new school." Her mother's voice cracked, but she held it together.

"So nice to meet you, young lady." Annabelle forced a smile and gently patted Izzie's shoulder. "It looks as if no one has followed you. Let's get you all inside and dried off from the rain. Mara is waiting for you inside."

Izzie took her mother's hand as the three of them followed Annabelle Grant. A tall redheaded man stood close by. He shut the gate behind them and followed them up the path. When they reached the school Izzie paused, staring up at the massive Georgian mansion in front of them. Izzie's mom tugged on her hand.

"Come on, sweetie, you'll be safe here."

They entered the huge foyer and Izzie looked around at the pictures and artifacts on the walls. The lamps flickered, throwing shadows across the floors, and a chill went up her spine. She wrapped her arms around herself and a hollow place began to build in the pit of her stomach. Annabelle Grant looked at Izzie's mother and father, knowing they had something to ask. Annabelle looked at Izzie and smiled.

"Why don't you follow our caretaker up to the guest bedroom and get changed into dry clothes? I just want a moment to speak to your parents."

Izzie looked at her mother, who put her hand on her shoulders. "We'll be right down here, okay? Go get changed."

Izzie nodded and looked at her father, who smiled. Her mother had tears in her eyes once more as she kissed her on the forehead. Izzie walked with the caretaker, looking back over her shoulder as her mother and father disappeared down the hall with Ms. Grant.

The headmistress, Mara Berens stood in the doorway

of her office, holding out her hand to wave the parents into her office.

"I'll take it from here Ms. Grant. Thank you." Mara followed the parents into her office, lighting the lamps, which cast a soft glow. She waved her hand to shut the door behind them and squeezed the mother's hand as she went past her. Izzie's mother turned to her husband and shook her head in exhaustion. He wrapped his arms around her and kissed her forehead.

"Everything will be all right."

She swallowed hard and the two sat in the tall-backed armchairs in front of Mara's desk, watching her closely.

"I am glad you brought her." Mara put her hands in her lap. "She will be safe here at the school."

Izzie's mother looked at her husband and back at Mara. "She will never really be safe, not with what she knows. They will keep coming for her, even here at the school."

Mara lifted an eyebrow. "What do you propose?"

The two sat quietly for a moment, then Izzie's father spoke up. "We want you to do a spell; an ancient one that will remove our memories. You know the one; I know you do. We want Izzie to forget us, and for her safety we will retain no memory of her either."

"That's too dangerous. You will cut her out of your life, and vice versa. She'll think she's an orphan. You could all be permanently damaged." Mara rattled off every reason she could think of, but she already knew what they would do.

"Better that than dead."

Mara leaned back in her chair and looked at the ceiling. She didn't want to do it; it was too risky—too out there. At the same time, she had come to know Izzie's parents and they weren't the kind of people who would suggest something like this unless they felt it was necessary. She shook her head and leaned forward to stare at the two of them.

"Are you sure there is no other way?"

"They will always be hunting us." Izzie's father looked at the floor. "Please, Mara! We would never ask if it weren't absolutely necessary."

Mara paused before nodding. "I'll do it, but she will stay here under my care until she graduates."

Tears rushed down Izzie's mother's face. "Thank you," she whispered.

"Thank you so much, Mara. Thank you." Her father reached across the desk to squeeze her hand.

"Do you want to say anything to her before I do this?"

"No" Izzie's father replied. "It's best we leave it like this."

Izzie's mother didn't question him. Mara stood up and walked around the desk to the two of them, motioning for them to stand. It would be the last time they would remember they ever had a daughter.

Izzie sat on a small padded bench and stared at her reflection in the mirror. She picked up the brush and ran it through her long dark hair, her eyes glowing. She had changed out of her wet clothes and was waiting for her mother. Everything had been so good; so perfect, then out of nowhere she was left wondering about her and her parents' future. A soft knock on the door drew her back to reality and she looked in the mirror, watching Mara's reflection as she walked inside and closed the door behind her.

"They're gone, aren't they?"

"Come, sit down next to me." Mara sat on the edge of the bed and patted the space next to her.

Izzie sighed, put down the brush, and moved to the bed. She was trying to be tough and hold back the tears, but they had *left*. They hadn't even said goodbye.

"Your parents are doing what is best for you, and though it kills them, they are saving your life."

"I feel like there is a hole in my chest." Izzie buried her face in her hands and let the tears flow.

"I know." Mara hugged her tightly, whispering into her ear, "But it will only last a minute."

Izzie slowly pulled back as she felt Mara's body getting warmer. She looked at her in confusion as her body glowed, the symbols running up and down her arms, flipping and fading away. Mara smiled, pursed her lips, and laid her hand on Izzie's head.

"*Erasus Preceding, Replacus the Meaning,*" Mara whispered as a broad line of light magic headed straight down her arm and over Izzie's head.

Mara pulled the memories from Izzie's mind, then sent a blue streak of light to fill the void with a false past. Izzie closed her eyes and fell back on the bed and Mara twisted the girl's orb into her hands, then turned toward the door.

"Come in," she called.

The caretaker entered slowly, looking from the orb to Izzie.

"She will need rest, but I want you to watch her. If she wakes before I return come get me immediately."

"Yes, ma'am," the caretaker replied, taking a seat in the chair next to the bed.

Mara pulled the covers over Izzie and looked at her for a moment before leaving the room and heading down to her office. She entered quickly, letting the large wooden door slam behind her, then went behind her desk and stared down at an etched wooden box. She took a deep breath, opened it, and set Izzie's memories between her mother's and father's. She closed the box and pulled out her wand, running it over the edges to seal it. She placed it on her shelf among the other artifacts and sat down in her chair.

Upstairs, tucked tightly in the guest bedroom, Izzie slept.

Streaks of light blew past Izzie's face, her dreams wild and vivid. Fireballs raced past her as she stood alone in the dark, wet alley. She looked around slowly, not feeling any danger but confused as to where she was, then the world around her began to curl into plumes of smoke. Flashes of laughter and faces she didn't recognize moved around her, then disappeared in the same smoky finality. When the smoke cleared she stood by herself in the dark.

She stepped forward, her shoes echoing into the vastness. She turned right and left, yelling into the void.

"Hello?"

No one answered as a chill ran through her and the hair on her neck stood on end. She stepped forward again, but this time her foot kept going and she fell into darkness. She landed with her eyes closed as her hands grasped the soft grass around her. She heard a laugh—a gentle soothing sound—and opened her eyes. Standing over her was a woman with long dark hair and the most beautiful smile. Her voice was kind and soft and Izzie couldn't help but smile.

"Wake up, Izzie."

Izzie tilted her head and the woman disappeared into a cloud of smoke that drifted off with the breeze.

"Izzie, time to wake up."

As the dream faded, Izzie slowly opened her eyes and looked at the high white ceilings. Her throat was dry when she tried to swallow, and she had to blink several times to get her eyes to focus. To the right was a voice; a familiar one.

"Good morning, dear." Mara smiled. "How are you feeling?"

Izzie looked at her and sat up, then rubbed her head and looked around the room. Everything was so fuzzy and confusing. "How did I get here?"

"Oh, silly!" Mara chuckled. "Remember? The orphanage placed you here as my ward. Do you know who I am?"

"Yes. Mara Berens, Headmistress."

"Exactly. Do you remember the orphanage?"

Izzie rubbed her head and looked down at the red and brown comforter. Slowly memories began to move through her mind, and before long her whole entire existence up to that point filled her brain. She could remember the orphanage and growing up there. She could remember her friends, the moment she found out she was a Light Elf, and receiving her scholarship to the School of Necessary Magic.

"Yes, I remember. Is this my room?"

"No." Mara laughed. "You will be placed in a room with four other girls, but you were here early so I set you up in the guest room. You can stay in this room whenever school isn't in session, if you like."

Izzie nodded and smiled, but felt like there was something else there, something she'd forgotten. Mara clapped her hands and set down a bag of clothes.

"These are your uniforms, my dear. Make sure they fit and rest today, because tomorrow is opening day for school. Lots to do—lots and lots. The kitchen is downstairs and they will serve lunch for us at noon, so don't be late."

"All right." Izzie nodded and Ms. Berens left the room in a hurry.

***

Mara closed Izzie's bedroom door and leaned against it for a moment, her face dropping. She had done a lot of magic in her day, both here and on Oriceran, but never in this manner. She felt for the girl.

"No time to feel pity, Mara. School starts tomorrow," she whispered to herself.

3

The morning sun cast shimmering rays of light over the rolling hills and green pastures of Albemarle County, Virginia. From the School of Necessary Magic, you could see for miles. It perched atop a lush green ridge, surrounded by hundreds of acres of pastures and forest. The school was tucked away from the traffic in nearby Charlottesville and gave just enough privacy to allow the students to flourish. It had been there for twenty years, and though the locals often wondered what went on out there, they never bothered to try to find out. Those who wandered near the iron gates found themselves wandering away, unable to remember what they were doing in that part of the county. It was the perfect setting for young talent to be molded into the future magical beings of Earth.

Local rumors said there was a spell over the entire school, but most chalked it up to overactive imagination.

The late summer heat was starting to simmer as students from all over the country flooded the grounds.

Some walked through magical portals with their parents in tow and others came in cars, just like the humans. Magical beings had been blending in with the communities for generations, but that was changing. Magic was very slowly returning to Earth.

"Hey, look what my dad got me for school this year!" a second-year wizard yelled, excitedly pulling out a brand-new wand.

"Thank God." his friend scoffed, rolling his eyes. "You almost burned down the west wing of the mansion last year when you sneezed."

"Yeah, I did it again at home. That's why the old man got me this one, made of evergreen broadleaf from my hometown." He smiled as he gazed at the twisted light wood.

"Oh yeah, you're a California boy." His friend chuckled. "Surf's up, bro."

The young wizard scrunched his nose. "Not really any surfing in Sacramento, bro."

"Well, show me what it can do. Conjure me up some breakfast. I missed it this morning." The kid rubbed his stomach and leaned back.

"All right," the young wizard replied, pushing up the sleeves of his uniform. "*Mountainus Bacon.*"

A plate appeared in the kid's lap and bacon began to pile up. "Whoa, awesome! Wait, that's enough, dude…seriously."

"Uh, I don't know how to stop it." The young wizard fumbled with his wand as the pile grew. "Shit!"

"Language, Mr. Lions," the headmistress caroled as she

passed them. She cast her elf energy outward and the plate disappeared. "Try studying instead of casting frivolously."

Mara Berens was in her nineteenth year as headmistress of the School of Necessary Magic. She was part Light Elf and part witch, with a touch of human heritage. She had a sense of humor, but definitely kept the kids under control. She believed in what the school had been organized to do, even if it the land and buildings were donated by Turner Underwood, the last Elf Fixer, and the school was started by the United States government. It was true that many of the kids who ended up there did so because they were a bit too much for normal society to handle, but it wasn't a place for truancy. It was a place for the most powerful magical teenagers to hone their skills so that when the gates opened between Earth and Oriceran once again they could help control the magic.

Izzie stood behind the headmistress and gave the young wizards a tight-lipped smile. The second-year stared down at his wand while the other sat on the picnic table and shoved bacon into his mouth.

Mara hurried through the crowds, pulling her wand out to stop the different spells the kids were casting. They had been pent up at home under the restrictions of magic in the real world and were now set free at the school. Mara tried to be understanding but it was inevitable that some mistakes would be made. She didn't want to end up with another fire in the schoolhouse as had happened the year before. Mara spotted Lucy Fowler, the Plants for Potions instructor, and scurried over. Lucy was older and had bright red hair that frizzed uncontrollably, and she wore wildly colorful outfits to match. She was a Light Elf with a particular proclivity for potions making.

"Lucy?" Mara hurried over. "Have you seen Miss Grant? She is supposed to be meeting with the new students' parents. I have a million and one things to take care of."

"She might be at the teachers' cottages still. She was trying to put together the last of her lesson plans. You know how much is constantly changing with the underground cities. The poor woman has an ever-evolving lesson plan."

Mara walked quickly to the back of the East Wing to look at the cottages below. She gave Izzie a wide-eyed glance before squinting into the valley—and there was Annabelle, carrying books stacked so high it took magic to keep them from falling. Mara sighed and sent out an orb carrying her message.

"Hurry, Miss Grant. The parents are gathering in the hall and you are to be introduced."

Annabelle looked up, startled by hearing the head-mistress' voice. She stopped waving her wand around the books and put her hand up to let Mara know that she was coming—and the books tumbled to the grass. She sighed and picked them up before heading to the double doors of the mansion.

The Georgian-style mansion sprawled across the grounds. It had wraparound porches and bright blue shutters, but on the inside were secrets and old magic from previous generations. Everything the young witches and wizards would need to learn was inside those doors, just waiting to be tapped. For the students, it was a place to increase their power, hang out with like-minded friends, and dream about the future. These weren't your typical teenagers, but it was a safe and respected place with instructors and teachers from both Earth and Oriceran.

After the car came to a stop in the circular drive a young first-year climbed out, straightening her plain gray tank top, even as her right Chuck Taylor sneaker was untied. She was petite and had olive skin, deep brown eyes, and white-tipped brown hair that cascaded over her shoulders. She clung tightly to the book in her arms as she scanned the souls that were bouncing around the grounds. Even though she was blind, she could tell there were many types of magical beings there. Magic had always been visible to her. Some were young, their powers hidden in swirls of colors, and others were more in control and confident in their magic. However, everyone, no matter what age or level, broadcast an undertone of excitement to be back at school.

This was Alison's first year at the School of Necessary Magic, and she was a bit nervous to meet everyone. She had recently lost both her parents. Her mother had been killed by an LA gang, and her father was killed in retribution for selling her mother out after he found out the truth about her and Alison. It had been a rough way to end the last school year. Alison was being dropped off by her new guardian, James Brownstone, a bounty hunter, and their friend Shay Carson, a field archaeologist. Neither were exactly parental types.

But they had both been there when she needed them,

rescuing her from a vicious death like her mother's. There was that other thing, too. Brownstone had explained that her mother was a two hundred and twelve-year-old Drow princess.

"You have the same abilities, Alison," he had told her.

"Not that I've noticed."

"Give it time. Your mother gave her life to keep you safe."

Too bad about dear old dad. That was the thing he wasn't saying.

"You must be Mr. Brownstone" a voice called. Alison was pulled back to the present and did her best to shake off the recent events. This place had to be better than all those deaths and lies and betrayals.

Alison turned and saw the bright green glow of Eleanor Hudson's aura. She watched the different streams of light float around the woman. She was a relatively powerful witch, but she kept that hidden and stayed in the background. She was a serious woman with a slight bit of whimsy, though Alison could tell she didn't let that show very often.

Eleanor adjusted her square black-rimmed glasses and pulled down on her black lace button-up top. Her blonde hair was pulled back into a loose but tidy bun at the nape of her neck and she smiled kindly at the young girl, years of trials creating wrinkles at the corners of her eyes. Mr. Brownstone had told her about Alison, but the girl was a little quieter than she thought she would be. "And Alison."

"Am I... supposed to bow or something?" James asked.

Shay slapped a hand to her forehead, rolling her eyes. "Seriously, Brownstone?"

The woman laughed and extended her hand. "How about I just offer you my hand? I'm Eleanor Hudson. I teach magical history and basic spells here. The headmistress was called away on an urgent matter, so she asked me to help Alison with her orientation."

They spoke a bit more, then Brownstone, Shay, and Alison made their awkward farewells and her new guardians left.

"Well, come on dear, no need to be shy, these students will never let you live it down."

Alison stepped forward and tripped over a small branch lying on the ground. All beings and all magic gave off energy, and that was how Alison saw the world. The rest were shadows, barely recognizable entities in the background. She smiled and looked toward Mrs. Hudson, getting her footing.

"I guess I should tell you that I see the world differently than others," Alison offered. "I see souls and energy. Oh, and spells. Most people don't even notice that I can't see."

"I may not have noticed either." Eleanor chuckled, withholding that she already knew. "Just a clumsy teenager like the rest." Eleanor put her arm around Alison's shoulder and walked her toward the large mansion. "Come on, let's get you familiar with the place. There is plenty of magic here, and probably more color than you've ever seen before."

Alison chuckled politely and walked beside Eleanor while scanning the students. She could tell the freshman from the upperclassman by the teal curiosity in their energy. She tried not to read any one person too deeply, since that would take her the rest of her time at the school.

"Ms. Berens, the headmistress, wanted to show you around, but as you can imagine there are a hundred things to do today so you are stuck with me."

Alison smiled and stopped to look at the energy of the large structure in front of her. Magic swirled around the building and the intertwined colors brought the structure of the house to life in her mind. It was unlike anything she had ever seen, and though it was exciting, the stream of dark magic mixed with the rest gave her a moment's pause. She had seen enough darkness in her life, even if it was in others' souls.

"Up ahead on your right is Max Regency. He will be your channeling teacher. He's a thoughtful man, full of human philosophy, and has a wealth of Oriceran and Earth knowledge. He spends a lot of time pondering with a glass of scotch."

Max Regency was a Gnome, standing around three feet in height. He wore suspenders and a tie, and almost always carried a rocks glass with something in it. He wasn't a drunk by any means, but Alison could tell from his energy's dark blue shade that he felt it made him look more intelligent and professor-like. She smiled, already knowing she was going to like him even if others found him boring.

"You will meet the rest of your teachers soon, but I want to get you familiar with the house." Eleanor walked Alison through the wooden double doors.

Alison looked around the entryway, watching the magic move and twist over the walls and artifacts and across the floor. She took a step toward a pillar to her right and touched the stone. There was old magic flowing deep beneath the bright new spells and protections that lit up the school. It was obvious the building had been there before it was a school.

Above them a vibrantly-souled creature flew through the open space. "That's our gargoyle." Eleanor looked up at the impressive creature. "Some witch brought him back from Oriceran and wasn't aware of just how dangerous he could be, so the new Fixer brought him here to live. He's friendly, but don't get in trouble or he'll carry you to the headmistress' office by your shirt."

"I'll try to remember that." Alison smiled.

She was in a whole new world, and though she had lived within magical energy her entire life, the school and the people inside were new to her. She imagined it was close to how everyone else saw the world, only they couldn't read everyone's personal energy like she could. Her nerves were still there, but they were lessening, and a sense of wonderment surged through her.

4

When the tour of the campus was done, they walked quietly through the foyer and back out onto the porch. Alison stayed close, but her eyes wandered over every inch of the space she was in searching for energy she could use to see the outline of her new world. Once outside, she stood by the steps, one arm wrapped around the column, staring out over the courtyard.

"All the older students are getting settled in their rooms. These are the first-year students like yourself." Mrs. Hudson smiled awkwardly and waved her hands. Alison could see the trails of energy following them. "Talk to people, and get to know them, I have some things to prepare before we head over for dorm assignments. Will you be all right on your own?"

Alison nodded in the direction of Mrs. Hudson's voice and the woman's energy took on a deep blue color—something she had seen many times. It was pity or sadness; the shades were similar, but both were irritating. Anyone who knew about her mother instantly changed to that shade, but Alison didn't want their pity. She had always been a confident girl, strong-willed, astute when it came to others, and well-spoken. However, when she was forced into a situation with new people she immediately started to feel uncomfortable. They all had so much to talk about. They'd lived normal lives, and Alison was the stray.

Still, she trusted Mr. Brownstone—she was having trouble thinking of him as "James"—and Shay, and though she had separated from them to go to school, they had promised her it was for the best. Now that she was here, Alison realized that there was a larger diversity of magical creatures on Earth than she had thought. Some of them she was seeing in her own unique way for the first time.

Alison glanced in the direction of Mara Berens voice. She was tending to another new kid and her obviously overbearing parents. Alison wanted to make friends, but this was all a bit overwhelming and she hung back as the others went in and out, chattering excitedly. Maybe she would end up with good roommates and that would break the ice.

Alison shook the thought from her mind as Ms. Berens walked swiftly through the crowd, warmly greeting all the new students. She was an interesting woman, outspoken and strict in a way Alison would imagine a grandmother to be. She liked order, not as a personal preference but to keep the school running smoothly. Anxiety bubbled through the headmistress' energy, but there was something more. Alison concentrated for a moment. There were threads of dark magic intertwined throughout. Although dark magic wasn't something to be feared in small doses—it balanced things— hers almost fought the light.

Alison had heard the rumors about Ms. Berens; that her daughter was a powerful elf, and that she herself had spent over a decade trapped in the World In Between. Alison shivered at the thought. That wasn't a place she ever wanted to visit, since it was the void between life and death. The living who slipped through the cracks were side by side with the dead who had been unresolved in life. They were able to watch everyone in the world, but they couldn't interact.

The hair stood up on the back of Alison's neck and she straightened. The other kids were gathering around the headmistress.

"All right, all right." Ms. Berens' voice rose above the others. "Welcome to the School of Necessary Magic. We are about to head inside for room assignments. Parents, you are welcome to stay as long as you'd like. Students, you may unpack, get ready for classes tomorrow, and venture around the manor. Dinner in the cafeteria will be served promptly at five. If you have any questions or concerns, I, along with several other instructors will be in the girls' dorm area, and our male instructors will be with the boys'."

The kids clapped intermittently as Alison took a step back, shoving her hands into her pockets and standing quietly to the side as the others moved toward the mansion. If she brought up the rear, she would be less likely to be forced into a conversation. The group moved up the winding staircase and down the hall. A young wizard read out loud, "D Wing, Second Floor NO BOYS ALLOWED".

"Well, that's a bummer." A young Light Elf giggled and gave Alison a mischievous nudge, jogging off to catch up with her parents.

Alison smirked, finding the girl's soul interesting. She could tell by the fiery red streaks that ran through the calm blue that the girl was outspoken and wild. Her parents' souls were exactly the same, only slightly more subdued. They all walked into a large living area that contained couches, a huge flat-screen tv, and vending machines. Surrounding them were sleeping rooms with identical doors and oil lamps on the wall, only there was no oil and the candle still flickered wildly.

Ms. Berens positioned herself in front of the TV. "I am going to call your names, and when I do, come up and collect your room number." She looked down at the clipboard, ignoring the excited murmur from the crowd.

Alison took a deep breath and gripped her bag's pink leather handle firmly. Everything she had in the world was in that one small bag, but that was okay because she no longer needed all the trinkets and toys she'd had as a child.

"Alison!" Ms. Berens called, looking at her with a smile and twinkle in her eye. "Well, come on."

Alison saw the delight in her soul as she pulled her suitcase to the front.

"Kathleen, Emma, Izzie, and Aya." The headmistress winked at Izzie as she quietly walked to the front and stood next to Alison.

Up came the wild girl from earlier, still emanating excitement. Behind her came another girl, her hands clenched tightly in front of her. Alison could tell she was nervous - there was a ripple rolling through her soul - but so was everyone else. The headmistress looked around for a moment and a short young woman stepped out from behind a group, her eyes pointed toward the floor as she walked up next to Izzie.

"All right, girls, your room is 314, to the right. Have fun," Ms. Berens stated, still watching Alison as they walked toward their room.

Kathleen got to the door first and dragged her bags in behind her. She stopped and put her hands on her hips, eyeing the five single poster beds with matching night-stands and dressers. "Definitely not the luxuries of home," she shrugged, "but better than I thought."

Aya and Izzie picked the beds closest to the door, neither of them looking at the others. Emma stayed quiet, her nerves shouting as she chose a bed in the center, leaving the two by the window. Kathleen grinned and threw herself onto one of them, then turned over on her back.

"I wonder how many brave Silver Griffins have laid on these beds?" she mused dreamily to no one in particular.

Alison laid her bag on her bed and pulled out a white zip-up hoodie. The old house was chilly compared to the hot sun beating down outside. Kathleen sat up and crossed her legs in front of her, leaning back on her hands. She looked from Alison to Emma to Aya and back again.

"I'm Kathleen." She was confident and loud, holding her chin high. "Light Elf from New York."

Emma looked up. "Emma, and I'm a witch." She was so quiet the girls could barely hear her.

"There's something else in you." Kathleen squinted, knowing she wasn't crazy.

Alison looked at Izzie, who was putting her clothes away in her dresser. As she turned around Alison noticed two empty spaces in Izzie's soul. She had never seen something like that before. Izzie smiled and turned back, forcing Alison's gaze to move to Emma's face.

"I'm also a Nicht," Emma replied more confidently than before.

"No way," Kathleen gasped. "That's really cool! Never met one before."

"What's a Nicht?" Alison asked.

Before Emma could answer Kathleen spoke up. "A magical being with bat-like wings, but they only come out when there is enough magic—like when you go to Oriceran."

"Neat." Alison smiled, giving Emma a kind look.

"How about you? And I LOVE those white tips. My mother would never let me do that." Kathleen twirled her red hair around her finger.

"I'm Alison." She smiled, thinking about her mother's long soft locks. She left out her magical abilities, not sure she wanted to have that conversation just yet.

"And how about you?" Kathleen asked, looking at the petite dark-haired girl by the corner bed.

The girl looked at Kathleen nervously. Alison could tell she was very shy and overwhelmed, but who wouldn't be around Kathleen? She was abrasive, to say the least, but Alison liked it. The Light Elf was someone who told it like it was.

"I'm Aya," she whispered in a soft voice, looking down at her hands.

Aya had a good soul, nothing damaged or odd, just a

quiet and calm light blue. Alison turned her gaze to the last girl in the room, the one she had seen walking around with the headmistress earlier that morning. She looked like she didn't want to talk but she knew Kathleen wouldn't let it go.

"I'm Izzie. I'm a Light Elf."

"Nice to meet you," Aya whispered, smiling quickly and turning away.

Kathleen bounced off her bed and stretched her arms in the air and her shirt rose to show her stomach. There was a star on her hip, surrounded by freckles. Aya looked away, trying not to stare.

"The freckles?" Kathleen laughed. "Curse of the red-headed child, I suppose. What kind of magical being are you, Aya?"

"A witch," she mumbled, opening her suitcase.

Kathleen narrowed her eyes. She sensed there was more to it but decided to let it be. They would know plenty about each other's powers soon enough. Alison sat down on the edge of the bed and kicked her suitcase underneath. Emma finished folding her shirts neatly and then did the same with her suitcase.

"We should explore. Get to know the campus so none of the older kids trick us with bad directions. I've heard they can be assholes." Kathleen had heard stories and was determined not to let them make a fool of her.

"I'm down." Emma shrugged.

"Sure." Alison shot her a tight-lipped smile.

"How about you, Aya?" Kathleen asked, walking over and plopping down on Aya's bed. "You want to explore this place with us?"

"I'll come with. Just let me finish unpacking."

Aya pulled a cherub doll from the bag, straightening its hair and setting it on top of the dresser. She pulled out another, then another, and kept going until she had eight dolls lined up perfectly next to each other. Kathleen raised an eyebrow.

"I use them for practice," Aya finally revealed, knowing she wouldn't get out of it. "Practice moving objects."

"But you're a witch." Kathleen laughed loudly, jumping down and putting her hands out in front of her. "It's easy-peasy."

White light flowed up from the ground, wrapped around Kathleen's body and shot from her hands. The door to the room opened wide with a bang. Kathleen smiled and turned around, dusting her hands.

"See?"

"Elf hands in your pockets, Kathleen," Ms. Berens bellowed from the hallway.

Kathleen hunched her shoulders and scrunched her nose, making the girls giggle, then smiled valiantly.

"Come on! So much to see, so little time."

5

The girls left the room, Kathleen in the lead, then Aya, Emma, and Alison, who found it easier to stay in the back in order to avoid questions about her sight. She didn't think she would have any issue since everything here was lit up like a Christmas tree. They walked down the hall and stopped to look at the half moon landing that ran around the staircase. There were three other hallways off that floor, but nothing was labeled.

"Anyone bring their map?" Kathleen asked.

The girls looked at each other for a moment, then Emma stepped forward and pulled out her wand. She waved it in a circle and light twisted, forming a map that floated in front of them. Kathleen nodded, impressed.

"That'll do." Kathleen rubbed her chin as she stared at the map. "Come on."

Kathleen walked fast, almost skipping toward the first hallway, then peered around the corner into the dark. As if the house could sense their presence, all the lamps lit along the corridor. The girls walked slowly to the end, where the only door in that hallway was located. Kathleen shrugged and slowly opened the large ornate wooden doors and the girls wandered inside, pausing to gaze in awe at the massive room.

Lining the walls were floor-to-ceiling shelves packed with books. Ladders rolled back and forth on their own, growing tall and then shrinking again to the bottom shelf. In the center of the room were empty tables and chairs for studying. Alison smiled, knowing she was going to be able to find any answers she needed in here. Ms. Berens had already assured her a spell was always in place and any book Alison opened would convert to Braille, and back again.

As the girls walked farther in there was a cough behind them.

They spun and everyone's eyes dropped to a small grumpy-looking Gnome with his arms crossed over his chest. He wore a suit and bowler hat with a red poppy on the brim that blew raspberries at the girls.

He narrowed his eyes and stepped forward, and the girls took a step back. "Busybodies," he grumbled. "Nothing for you to see in here today. And don't even think about taking a book. I'll know."

Izzie moved closer to Alison, giving her a nervous glance.

"Who...who are you?" Emma swallowed hard, not wanting to be in trouble on her first day.

The Gnome stood up a bit taller. "Leo Decker, your head librarian and keeper of knowledge at the school.

You'll be glad to remember that too. Now, go on! Get out of here."

Leo was gruff, as Gnomes tended to be. His people were the keepers of artifacts and also protected the books in the Light Elf mansion in Oriceran. Gnomes were known to be excellent secret-keepers but they were also loners, sticking to their own kind and fearlessly protecting their charges. Even Kathleen didn't have the nerve to talk back to him.

The girls nodded and scurried out of the library and the door slammed behind them. Kathleen looked at the map in front of her and shook her head, and Emma bit her bottom lip and looked at the others.

"Did you see that the library had a vault?"

"I did. Must be books for the professors or something." Alison didn't think much of it.

"I don't understand why libraries full of old dusty books are even necessary." Kathleen rolled her eyes and patted her bag. "I mean, seriously…didn't the iPad make that obsolete?"

"They don't have iPads in Oriceran." Emma looked away quickly, hoping she didn't piss Kathleen off.

"They will when they come here." Kathleen pointed to a spot on the map. "Next thing you know, we are going to find an old set of Encyclopedia Britannicas lying around."

The girls giggled at Kathleen and headed back down the staircase, taking a right on the bottom floor to enter the West Wing. There were paintings and sculptures everywhere and magical energy clung to everything. Alison wondered whose magic it was but didn't bring it up since the girls couldn't see magic the way she did. The West Wing was the main teaching area, full of classrooms with whiteboards, desks, and all kinds of interesting artifacts. On the right side of the wing was a massive IT center packed with the newest computers and technology. The school felt it was imperative for the students to learn human technology, given the way the future was headed. Everyone would need to learn the ways of the humans, even though magic was easier.

The girls crossed the foyer and headed to the East Wing, where there was a well-equipped gym with treadmills, weights, and even some weapons for sparring. Attached to that was an indoor pool with tall cement diving boards. Alison loved the idea of swimming; she'd done it all the time with her mother. Just the thought of her mom brought a pang to her chest, but she shook it off and kept moving. Aya noticed her sad face but looked away quickly.

The second floor held the first and second-year dorms and the library they'd already located so they headed up to the third floor, stopping abruptly when a third-year with a clipboard stepped forward and put his hand out. Kathleen looked him up and down, pegging him immediately as a suck-up.

"Upperclassman dorms, no newbies allowed." He cleared his throat, still staring down at his clipboard as magical symbols appeared on the page. "Cafeteria is on the bottom floor, North Wing. The entrance is behind the staircase."

"Behind the stairs?" Kathleen asked with a chuckle.

"This house is bigger than you think." The boy flashed a mischievous grin and Kathleen wrinkled her nose.

The girls headed back down and peeked behind the staircase, where they found locked double doors. On one was a sheet of paper listing the cafeteria's hours.

"There are stables here." Izzie looked at Emma, whose eyes lit up. "With horses we can ride."

"Really?" Aya's eyes brightened and for a moment she forgot just how uncomfortable she was.

"You can learn to care for all types of Earth creatures here in your second year. Like a veterinarian, only when you get farther into the program you start learning about magical creatures too." Izzie couldn't remember where she'd heard that, but it must have been in the orphanage.

"That's awesome." Aya smiled.

"I'm not an outdoorsy kind of girl." Kathleen waved away a fly in front of her. "But I've heard the barn is used for more than just horse care, if you know what I mean." Kathleen waggled her eyebrows and Aya looked at her with confusion, while Emma's cheeks turned bright red. Alison just chuckled, knowing exactly what she meant—and made a mental note to stay away from the stables. Boys weren't on her radar, not after everything she had gone through.

The girls went outside and consulted the map again: the stables were at the bottom of the ridge, reached by a winding trail. They walked through the green grasses of the pastures, where the caretaker was training one of the horses.

"I wonder if we could take one of these beauties for a ride down to the pond on our time off?" Kathleen shooed away another fly and looked into the distance.

"The pond is off-limits during the school week," Aya pointed out quietly.

"So is doing magic outside the classrooms but that doesn't stop anyone." Kathleen scoffed.

"You've been here five minutes and you're already planning to break the rules." Emma giggled.

"Hell, yeah." Kathleen smiled. "Come on, there are the stables."

The girls wandered through the stables, although Kathleen wrinkled her nose at the smell of manure. Aya walked right up to the horses and petted them, almost as if she understood what they were thinking. Alison could see their souls, and though they were just regular Earth creatures there was calm and kindness in their energy. They let Aya take her time while listening to Kathleen gossip about the upperclassmen.

"I saw some pretty hot guys, but I have a boyfriend back home." Kathleen shrugged nonchalantly. "He's out of school; works for a wand-maker. How about you?"

Emma looked at Kathleen and sighed. "My parents won't let me date until I'm sixteen."

"Lame, but what happens in school they don't have to know about."

Kathleen winked at Emma and focused her attention on Aya. She was trying to get the girl to break out of her meek and quiet little shell. Alison just watched her performance in amusement, knowing there was more to Aya than met the eye.

"How about you, Aya? Have any hottie back in... Where are you from?"

"Georgia." Aya blushed and looked down. "And yes, I have a boyfriend. Henry."

"Really?" Kathleen was genuinely shocked. "How long

have you been together?"

"Three years, but we've been best friends our whole lives."

"Oooh," Kathleen teased. "Are you, you know, sneaking off for some hanky-panky?"

"No." Aya was mortified, but she quickly wiped her expression, not wanting Kathleen to poke fun at her anymore. "I mean, we've talked about it, but...I don't know. I want to wait."

"Noble," Kathleen grumped. "And boring. How about you, Alison? Your parents keep a lock on your chastity belt too?"

"No." Alison chuckled. "I've just been busy. No time for that."

Kathleen looked at her strangely but didn't question it any further. She could tell there was a lot to Alison; much more than she was willing to say. Kathleen took a deep breath and pushed herself off the post as the barndoor swung open. Two upperclass girls, Scarlett, a Light Elf, and Claire, a witch, strolled in. They stopped and eyed the freshmen.

"Look, Scarlett, fresh meat." Claire laughed.

Claire's hair was pulled into two low ponytails, each side a different color. Her makeup was thick, and she wore a perfectly-pressed skirt, tight tank top, and flat leather sandals. Draped around her neck was a sheer Versace scarf, and jewels dangled from her wrists. She had her own style, that was for sure, and everything was high-end. She sneered at Izzie, looking her up and down before turning to Scarlett.

"Looks like they brought in weak ones this year." Scarlett scoffed. "We'll come back later and check on your horse. Let the newbies run wild."

The girls laughed and left, slamming the barn door behind them. Kathleen unclenched her teeth and looked down at her fingernails.

"Who were *they*?" Emma asked, crossing her arms over her chest.

"Upperclassmen." Kathleen rolled her eyes. "Claire, the one with the purple and blue hair? She has more money than the king of Oriceran. Her family is loaded, and she drove in here this morning in a brand-new Mercedes. She's kind of a bitch."

Alison had quietly scanned their souls and energy. Claire without a doubt had an attitude, but her energy radiated something much different than arrogance: confusion, anxiety, and an unknown something Alison couldn't put her finger on. She was insecure but didn't allow it to show on the outside—not like Emma, who was sweet but definitely trying to impress Kathleen.

"She's so confident." Emma pouted. "I wish I could be like that—walk into a room and not feel nervous."

"Me too," Aya whispered. There was wistfulness in Aya's energy.

"And be obsessed with objects instead of people?" Alison shook her head in disgust.

"Not me." Izzie glanced at Alison and scuffed her shoes through the hay on the floor.

"I'd kill for those platforms in baby blue." Kathleen shrugged. "Being like that will make your life go a lot easier here. It's just like everywhere else—a hierarchy, where the strong take control and the weak are eaten."

6

When the girls were done in the stables, they walked back to the pasture and tried to decide what to do next. There was still an hour or so before dinner, and Alison, like the other girls didn't want to just go back and sit in their dorm room. Kathleen tapped her hands against her sides and a telltale grin moved across her lips.

"Let's compare our magic. Since we'll be sharing a dorm all year we might as well know what each other is capable of."

"All right..." Emma was obviously unsure, but not willing to let on.

"Why not?" Aya replied with a shy smile.

"I'll go first." Kathleen stood up straight, putting her hands down next to her, and stuck out her chest.

She closed her eyes and pulled the energy from the ground beneath her feet. Her eyes glowed and Oriceran symbols turned and moved on her arms. She breathed deeply through the warmth of the energy, willing it into the palm of her hand. She rolled an orb of light in her hands, whispering so quietly they couldn't make out what she said. The symbols dimmed slightly, molding the shape of the energy.

She opened her still-glowing eyes and held out her palm, where the orb shifted into a rose, then slowly morphed into a butterfly. The butterfly took flight, whizzing around the girls to land on Alison's shoulder for just a moment before flying over their heads again. The girls could feel the warmth of Kathleen's magic in the butterfly as it touched them, then it finally returned to her palm and fizzed apart in a cascade of sparks. The symbols on Kathleen's arms disappeared and she smiled proudly.

"My mom taught me that one." Kathleen pursed her lips and looked at the girls. "All right, Emma, let's see what you can do."

Emma pulled out her wand and cleared her throat.

"Wait, do something with your wings." Kathleen raised her eyebrows.

"I can't. Not enough magic, even here." She shrugged. "Maybe when we all get a little stronger. We'll see."

Kathleen sneered and stepped back as Emma focused and tapped the long slender wand with her index finger, trying to decide what to do. A smile moved across her face and she swirled her wand over her head, streaks of orange light trailing it.

"*Venus Stargaze*," Emma murmured, letting the light out of her wand.

The girls twisted and turned as the light shot around them and gathered, then started rotating slowly. Motes of light dotted the air until a complete map of the constellations was visible above them. Kathleen pushed her finger through one of the glowing stars and the magic wrapped around her thumb.

"That's pretty neat." Aya smiled as Emma swirled her wand again causing the solar system to disappear into the wind.

"Cool," Kathleen replied, unimpressed. "Okay, Aya, your turn."

She pulled out her wand and looked at a tall statue on the edge of the field. Alison didn't see any energy transferring into the wand and she looked at her curiously. Aya stared hard at the statue, gripping her crooked dark wand tightly. The tip lit and the statue began to tremble, then rose slowly off the ground and swayed heavily in the air. Alison still couldn't see any energy in the wand. There was something different about Aya's magic.

Slowly she lowered the statue and as she relaxed the end of her wand went dark again. Kathleen and Emma clapped, smiling widely. Moving large objects with magic seemed benign, but they all knew it took extreme control of your powers—something most seniors struggled with. Aya put her head down and smiled shyly, glancing quickly at Alison.

Nervous energy bubbled in Alison's stomach; she didn't *know* what she could do. That was what she was here to learn. She'd done what research she could, but the information was scarce. She knew there was strong magic inside of her, and since her hair was slowly turning white, she knew that it was growing.

"All right, Alison. You're up." Kathleen looked at her curiously.

"I'm going to admit something, so don't laugh. I'm here to learn what my magic is. I don't know yet what I can do. Please don't ask me anymore about it right now." She lowered her eyes, scuffing a foot as she stepped on the untied shoelace.

They all looked at her curiously and Kathleen took a breath to speak, then let it out. "I know what you are. I saw Drows on trips to Oriceran. They're both feared and revered, and unknown on Earth. It's cool."

Alison lifted her chin in surprise, smiling at Kathleen because she just accepted that Alison wasn't going to do anything.

Kathleen turned to Izzie. "Last but not least! Show us what you got, Izzie."

"Okay..." She pulled the energy from beneath her feet and a light trickle of magic moved up to her finger. A white beam shot out and swirled around Alison's leg and down to her untied shoelace. The lace twisted and turned and finally made a perfect bow.

"That's it?" Kathleen had expected more.

"I don't know a lot of magic yet. It wasn't a big deal in my family."

"What, are you Amish or something?" Kathleen giggled, losing interest.

Izzie wasn't going to tell the girls she was from an orphanage yet. Alison moved closer to her and smiled, looking down at her shoe.

"Thanks."

"No problem. Wouldn't want you tripping over something. Kathleen would never let you live it down."

The two girls looked at Kathleen, who was talking to

Emma about her extensive travels and all the boys she had dated. Izzie and Alison giggled softly.

"We all have history we don't want people to know," Alison murmured softly. She shrugged. "My mom died recently."

"Really?" Izzie suddenly didn't feel so alone. "I don't remember mine."

Something in Izzie's soul was off, but Alison let it go, figuring there was stuff she wasn't ready to share—a feeling that was all too familiar.

"Where to now?" Alison asked, catching up to Kathleen who once again was in the lead.

"I heard there's a stream around here somewhere. I also heard it has a tire swing and a mossy area just to chill. It's like an escape for the students, but I'm not sure what direction to go in." Kathleen looked across the property.

At the top of the hill to the left of the pasture was the groundskeeper, his wild red hair blowing in the wind. He ran one hand across the horse's head, feeding it a carrot with the other. There was a broken-down tractor next to him, and tools spread across the grass. Horace Rigby had been at the school for years, but there was nothing magical about him. He was just a normal human from Austin, Texas. He had lived there with his mother and spent a lot of time with his Aunt Estelle when he was younger. She owned a bar out there and was one of the few humans who had known about Oriceran's magic long before it had started to seep out into the open.

He had been standing there watching the girls play with their powers. He knew more about it than most Earth-side witches and wizards. He could remember Aunt Estelle feeding him Nachos at her patio bar when he was a kid. She had told him stories about magic on Earth with her cigarette hanging from her lip and her bright red bouffant that never seemed to change. It wasn't until he was older that he had realized the stories were true.

"Excuse me." Kathleen smiled as the girls walked up to Horace. "You're Mr. Rigby, right?"

"Just Horace." He nodded at them. "Groundskeeper here."

"What exactly does a groundskeeper do?" Emma asked.

"Well, I take care of the mansion and the property and I exercise the horses and other animals out here. Anything to do with keeping grounds up."

"That would make sense." Emma's cheeks grew bright red.

"I also tend to the foreign plants and animals that come and go from here," he added.

"Foreign?" Emma asked.

"Yeah, like plants and animals from Oriceran." He squinted into the sky as a gargoyle flew over them. The girls stepped closer together, since none of them were used to gargoyles. They'd only heard stories about them as children. "That one may look scary, but he is kind of fun to be around. Came to me when he was just a baby. Looks like he is following you girls."

"Great, just what we need. A gargoyle tail." Kathleen grimaced. "I've seen them in my trips through the portal with my mother. They didn't seem so friendly over there."

"He's a bit gruff, and he's sneaky like gargoyles tend to be, but you don't need to be afraid of him."

Alison stared at his soul for a moment, realizing there was no magical energy around him—just the light-yellow human type. She hadn't imagined there would be humans working at the school, though it shouldn't really surprise her. Humans had *founded* the school, after all. She wondered what it was like for him to work every day among a bunch of magical teenagers.

"Would you be able to point us in the direction of the stream?" Kathleen asked. "We wanted to check it out before dinner is served."

Horace looked at the valley below. "Sure. You see down there where the teachers' cottages are?"

"Yes."

"Don't go there. It's off-limits," Horace snapped.

"Good to know." He could almost see Aya make a mental note, but Kathleen didn't flinch.

"But if you go to the bottom of this hill and skim along the edge, you'll see the start of it. Just follow it back into those woods. It's pretty easy to find the student's hangout area. They've been going there for years. There's a long row of purple pansies that bloomed in the moss this summer, which is like a trail back to the tire swing."

"Right." Kathleen nodded and followed the trail with her eyes. "Thanks, Horace."

He kept a straight face as Alison walked by. He wondered what kind of energy he gave off. He'd been told that she was a Drow before the semester had begun, but no one really talked about them. He nodded at Izzie, who gave him a half-smile, clearly remembering him from when she had woken up in the mansion the first morning.

The girls headed for the stream, chattering about their lives back home. Alison listened but said nothing, much like Izzie. Their lives all seemed so normal, but Alison's… Well, it was a lot more complicated than she wanted to admit. Hopefully things would get better now that she was in school, but at least now she had Shay and Mr. Brownstone.

7

Peter, shirtsleeve torn, hair ruffled, and soot smeared across one cheek, tripped over a log as he ran through the woods. He windmilled his arms to steady himself and he flung a ball of magic from his wand. Ethan jumped to the side and landed in a pile of wet leaves, the orb barely missing his shoulder. It struck an old dead tree and the branch exploded, turning to sawdust that covered his head.

"Jesus, watch what the hell you're doing!"

Peter looked at the pile of sawdust on Ethan's head, dumbstruck. "I'm so sorry. It just went off on its own."

"Shhh." Ethan put his finger to his lips, hearing footsteps.

Just then a beam of light blew through the woods, knocking the leaves from the trees above them. They showered down like a hard rain, covering the boys. They ran, dodging in and out of cover, jumping over roots and fallen trees and over the ridge that led to the stream.

"The clearing is just ahead," Peter shouted to Ethan.

"Great, even *less* cover."

When the boys made the clearing, they slid down the embankment, then hopped up and dusted off their pants. Ethan looked back at the woods but saw no sign of the older kids yet. They noticed Alison and the rest of the girls, and Peter smiled awkwardly as he picked leaves from his hair.

"What the hell?" Ethan growled angrily. "I'm here five minutes and I'm running from punks like I was still at home."

Ethan was tall and fit and his hair was short on the sides with a tuft of curls on the top. His bright green eyes almost glowed as he looked wildly around for any sign of the older boys. He was used to being chased; he was a half-wizard, half-Light Elf who had been living on the streets until he was brought to the school.

Peter, on the other hand—a wizard descended from one of the first to come to Earth—*wasn't* used to the chase. He was a nerdy kid who had grown up in the suburbs and had been obsessed with science when he was little. After coming into his powers, he'd figured out that he could mix science with magic and usually come up with even more powerful spells. The only problem was, they didn't always work out the way he thought they would. For that reason, he could almost always be found with a swipe of soot or burn mark on his clothes. His parents figured it would be better to send him to the school where he could learn to create safely, than eventually watch him blow himself up in the basement.

"We are trying to have a nice quiet time here before dinner. What are you two idiots doing out here, and why do you look like you were attacked by a troll?" Kathleen put her hands on her hips and raised her eyebrows.

"And smell like it too." Emma wrinkled her nose and leaned back on the rock she was sitting on.

"Oh, tie it up." Ethan scoffed. "We don't need the girls on our ass too."

"Excuse me, but I can promise you I am nowhere near..." Kathleen waved her hands, a disgusted look on her face. "'Your ass' as you put it."

Ethan looked at Alison and smiled awkwardly; he still had twigs and debris stuck in his hair. Alison lifted her eyebrows and gave him a half-smile, unsure what to make of the whole scene. Suddenly two more boys ran up to them, laughing and looking down at Ethan and Peter.

"There you are, idiots."

"Oh, great, more of them." Kathleen threw her hands up and rolled her eyes. "And who are the two of you, since these two don't have any manners?"

"Wyatt." The tall dark-skinned boy gave a toothy grin and bowed. "Wood Elf at your service, and this is my best friend Henry."

Henry had bright blue eyes, shaggy blond hair and a smile that made Kathleen stare. He was stylin', wearing a football jersey, straight-leg jeans, and Chuck Taylors. Alison could see his soul so she knew he didn't have magical powers, but he was definitely not human.

"And what are you?" Kathleen was tight-lipped.

"Shifter."

Wyatt slapped him on the back. "And a damn mean one."

Wyatt had regular magical abilities. He was a rich kid who came from a long line of Wood Elves and had grown up in the lap of luxury not too far away. He rarely gave a crap about the rules, especially when it came to lower-classmen.

Henry was, a total jock, interested in every sport under the sun. It was what kept him from falling into the shifter crowd, the ones no one at the school took seriously. Wyatt and Henry had roomed together their first year and been inseparable ever since, especially when it came to torturing newbies.

Wyatt turned his attention to Peter and Ethan, who stood to the side with their wands out, still trying to catch their breath. Ethan was scowling and gripped his wand tightly. Alison could see the angry energy radiating from him, while Peter was more frightened. Ethan hated being bested, especially when it was by two idiots picking on the new kids.

"Come on, boys, we were just having a little bit of fun. Right, Henry?"

"Oh yeah, just a bit of fun with the street rat and his mad-scientist friend."

Ethan gritted his teeth and balled his fists. "I'm not a street rat, and I barely know this kid. We share a room."

Wyatt swung his arm over Henry's shoulder and leaned his head back. "Ahh, the memories. Remember when we were new freshy roommates?"

Henry chuckled. "And we tied those two upperclassmen upside down to a tree somewhere out here?"

"Sounds good to me." Ethan gripped his wand tighter.

Izzie sighed and shook her head, not understanding boys and their constant need to prove they were bigger and stronger than everyone else. She couldn't remember being around boys before; her orphanage had been all girls. Kathleen, however, knew exactly what it was like, having grown up in coed private schools.

"Tell everyone where your parents are right now." Henry smiled proudly.

"Belize. Our chauffeur dropped me and Henry off at school, of course."

"It was a Mercedes. What did you come in on, Ethan? Oh, that's right—the school sent the groundskeeper to pick you up. The human."

Both Wyatt and Henry laughed loudly, irritating everyone at the stream. Kathleen wasn't impressed, and even Aya looked like she wanted to throw a little magic their way. Ethan had had enough, though. He couldn't bite his tongue any longer. He had promised to behave while he was here, but the injury these boys were causing was almost too much to bear.

Alison made her way over to Ethan and put her hand on his shoulder. "It's not worth it."

"Sure it is. These two assholes need someone to teach them a lesson. Why not me? Just a little zap to make it hard for them to walk for a couple of days."

"And you'll be in detention when school hasn't even started."

Ethan glanced at Alison, noticing she didn't make eye contact with him. He shook his head and shrugged her hand off, then raised his wand up. Wyatt smacked Henry in the stomach and nodded in Ethan's direction and both laughed even louder. Ethan breathed heavily and snarled. He swirled his wand over his head and shot out a steady stream of purple light. Wyatt and Henry grabbed each other and looked up as the energy snapped a large limb high in the tree above them.

Wyatt shook his head. "Shit, come on man. Let's get out of here."

Wyatt and Henry took off through the woods, running as fast as they could. Alison stepped away from Ethan and raised her shoulders. The limb plummeted to the ground, crashing hard and rolling over the edge of the ledge. Ethan put his wand in his pocket and nodded firmly at Peter.

"You gotta get that wand in check. You almost took my head off back there."

Peter nodded, and Emma got up and looked over the edge into the gully with a smirk.

"Personally, I think you handled those bullies just right. I don't care if you are an upperclassman, rich, a jock—whatever—you don't get to treat people that way."

"Exactly." Ethan nodded again, finally noticing his surroundings. "Hey, this is a nice area. I'll have to come down here for some R&R."

Kathleen threw her hands up and plopped down on a rock, and Ethan looked at her with a raised eyebrow. Peter walked to the edge of the stream and cupped a hand to scoop up some water. He pulled his wand out and swirled it around his hand, and a tiny water fairy danced across his hand for a moment before splashing back into the stream.

Izzie smiled. "That's really cool."

"It's just using the elements and magic together, that's all." Peter shrugged, proud but not wanting to show it.

Emma was still standing at the edge of the gulley and looking down to where the branch had hit. Her attention had been caught by something sparkling below. It looked like a hole, maybe a cavern or something, that the branch had broken through. The sides shimmered with black stones, and it gave off a magical glow that was hard to ignore.

She waved at the others. "Hey guys, check this out. I think that branch punched through something. It looks like an underground cave or something."

The girls walked over and peered over the edge. Ethan narrowed his eyes, wondering if it was another trick, strolling over only after he saw Peter's eyes widen. Emma was right; there was some sort of cavern below, and the hole was big enough for them to fit through. He was always up for a little exploring, but from the look of most of the girls, he wasn't sure *they* would be.

"I wonder what's down there." Kathleen looked curious, but couldn't imagine actually crawling down there to check it out. As she had said before, she wasn't a nature girl. The walk through the woods and the mossy patch by the stream was about as adventurous as she got.

Alison realized that for the first time that day she didn't feel awkward in the group. They were all acting normal around each other, like they had been friends for years. Their energy had calmed, something she hadn't been sure would happen—except for Peter, who looked nervous.

"Let's check it out."

Kathleen turned to Alison in surprise. "Uh, *no*. I am not going in there."

"I will." Emma raised her hand.

Izzie nodded at Alison. "Me, too."

Alison turned to Ethan with a smile. "How about you?"

"Hell, why not? I've *slept* in worse places than that."

8

E than was the first one down, taking a leap over the edge and landing firmly in the leaves. Peter climbed down awkwardly and reached up to help Emma. Izzie looked at Alison and shrugged, then sat down and slid into the gulley. Aya went next, taking Ethan's hand, her cheeks growing rosy red. Alison looked at Kathleen, whose energy showed she was pissed, then took Ethan's hand and jumped down. Kathleen sighed and mustered enough magic to slowly float her down into the gulley.

"Why does it not surprise me that I am climbing down into the depths of hell with you guys?"

Alison smiled and walked to the opening, feeling for the edge of the stone stairs with her foot. She glanced at Izzie, whose energy was radiating curiosity, and shrugged again, stepping into the hole. One by one they entered, slowly making their way down while being careful not to touch anything.

Izzie stopped at the bottom. "Can someone throw up a light?"

Ethan swirled his wand, sending out several bright orbs that skipped along the walls before planting themselves like lanterns. "That should help."

Izzie ducked to pass through an earthen arch. After a few steps she stopped, her mouth dropping open as she looked at the immense damp cavern. Black crystals shimmered along the walls and stalactites jutted from the ceiling, water dripping from them into pools. Kathleen pushed ahead and stood next to Alison, crossing her arms.

"Well, this is homey."

"I think it's an adventure."

Kathleen snorted and looked across the cavern, squinting at something in the back corner. A crack in the roof let through just enough light for the object to be illuminated by the sun. Izzie and Kathleen looked at each other for a moment before walking over, being careful where they stepped. Alison could see the bright energy that emanated from the object, but the colors moved so fast she couldn't read what it was. Kathleen gasped as they stopped.

Alison still couldn't make out what the object was. "What is it?"

"It's an egg of some sort."

Ethan came up beside them and stared down at the black egg whose specks of gold flickered in the sunlight. Kathleen looked back, only to find the others hadn't moved from the archway, not willing to come in any farther. She rolled her eyes and sniffed.

"Cowards."

Ethan sighed and stepped back, putting up his hands. "I

think they might have the right idea. We should get out of here."

"No way!" Kathleen bent down in front of the egg, mesmerized by the swirling gold specks. "We should take this back to the mansion; see what comes of it."

"Are you *nuts*?" Ethan shook his head and waved his hands. "I've never seen anything like it. Who knows what kind of crazy creature will come bounding out of that thing."

Kathleen started to reach forward but stopped as Alison reached out, grabbing her arm and gave her a look advising caution. Kathleen nodded, and against Alison's better judgment she slowly let go of Kathleen's arm.

Kathleen stepped forward and put both hands on the egg, feeling a surge of energy in her gut. She smiled, looking around before carefully picking up the egg and pausing for a reaction. Ethan looked around as well, but nothing happened.

"You guys are a trip." Kathleen laughed. "What do you think this is, Indiana Jones? Trust me, there aren't any booby traps."

Ethan shook his head and walked back to the others. Alison gently gripped the egg, unsure what to do next. "You can put it in my backpack so you aren't walking through the mansion with a random black and golden egg in your hands."

"Good idea." Kathleen gently turned Alison around and slipped the egg into her bag. Its energy flowed through the fabric and into Alison's chest, giving her a warm sensation. She still couldn't sense what the object was or if there was anything inside, but she suddenly felt the need to take it back to their room and protect it.

"All right, it's in there." Kathleen dusted her hands off and took one last good look around the cavern to make sure there were no more. "Let's get this thing back to our room and hide it. We don't need Ms. Berens to snatch this baby right out from under us."

"Kathleen?"

"Yeah?"

"Did you feel..."

"Feel what? The ungodly need to protect the thing? Yeah, but keep it between us. I don't need the other ones running off to Berens."

"Right."

Kathleen put her hands up in victory and headed for the arch. Alison tightened the straps on her pack and followed her voice, bringing up the rear as they walked back through the tunnel and climbed into the light. When they reached the top, the sun was starting to sink in the sky.

"We should get back, get this hidden, and get to the cafeteria for dinner. It'll look suspicious that all of us are late on our first day here."

The guys climbed out of the gully first and pulled up Emma and Aya, then did the same for Izzie and Alison. Kathleen refused their help, using magic to get her up and out. Kathleen ran to the front of the group, leaving Izzie and Alison to bring up the rear.

Izzie looked curiously at Alison, eyeing her bag. "Are you sure it's safe to have that thing in there? I mean, we have no idea what it is."

"I think so," Alison replied, feeling carefully with her foot as she took each step. "I don't feel or see anything harmful in its energy." She had no idea what was inside that thing, if anything, but she wanted to calm Izzie's nerves…and she *definitely* didn't want her to freak out and tell the headmistress. It was obvious she knew her pretty well.

When they reached the mansion Ethan and Peter headed to their dorm and the five girls went to their wing, listening to the announcement from the intercom.

"All students should wear their uniforms to the cafeteria for dinner," Ms. Berens stated. "This is an assembly to meet and greet. Dinner will begin in approximately fifteen minutes."

The girls sped up, trying to keep blank faces so that they wouldn't draw too much attention. One by one they filed into their room, Izzie closing the door behind them. Kathleen pulled the egg out of Alison's backpack and the girls gathered closely. All eyes were wide as Emma reached out to touch the stone-like object.

Kathleen slapped her hand away. "No need to put you in danger too. Alison and I have already touched it, but we have no idea what it is. Best keep a safe distance unless you absolutely have to pick it up."

"I have to agree." Alison shook her head, looking down at the deep blue energy clinging to her hands.

Kathleen surveyed the room. They had to hide it somewhere good; somewhere no one would think to look. Finally, she walked over and opened Alison's top drawer, pushing her panties and socks to the sides. Alison frowned. She knew from the sound where Kathleen was rummaging.

"Why can't it be *your* underwear drawer?"

"Because my drawer has a lot of designer clothes, including my lingerie. I'm not putting an egg in there and having it hatch on my unmentionables."

"And *mine* are okay?"

"I'll make you a deal: if it hatches on your stuff I'll take you shopping."

Alison raised an eyebrow, but knew Kathleen wasn't going give in. "Fine."

Kathleen carefully set the egg down and stood back, watching as if it was suddenly going to do something. After a few moments of nothing, Alison pushed her socks around it, creating a sort of nest. Carefully she shut the drawer, putting her finger in the opening to make sure she was leaving it just a smidge cracked for light. Kathleen nodded happily and went over to her closet, pulling out a perfectly-pressed uniform. Alison reached into her wardrobe and felt across the hangers for the third one. She had a system that helped her get ready without mixing plaids with a floral print. She pulled out her own uniform, as Kathleen came over and dusted hair off the front for her. "That's better."

Kathleen's energy showed she wasn't happy at having to wear a uniform, but Alison didn't really care. It was what it was, and at least she would have some sort of uniformity with the others at the school—something she wanted in order to stay under the radar.

When she had finished getting dressed, she smoothed her button-up blouse and pulled the blue cardigan tighter around her shoulders. Her skirt came to just above the knee and her socks were pulled up her calves. She slipped her feet into her brand-new loafers and ran her hands over her hair, unable to see what she looked like—not that she ever had. Across the room the other girls were dressing, and Izzie pulled her hair back in a low ponytail. She glanced at Kathleen, who had rolled her skirt halfway up her thigh. Izzie rolled her eyes and pulled on her cardigan, nodding at the others.

It shocked Izzie that even though they were all dressed the same, they each had their own flair. Alison's was Chuck Taylors, Emma had a rainbow pin on her sweater, Aya buttoned her blouse all the way to the top, and Kathleen, well, she *was* her own flair. Izzie didn't have anything extra, but that was the way it had always been for her, it seemed.

Kathleen finished up in the mirror and walked to the center of the room, swaying her red hair back and forth. "All right, ladies, if we are going to keep an egg in a drawer in our room, we need assurance from each person that this will stay between us."

Emma glanced up. "I'm not gonna say anything."

Izzie nodded, glancing at Alison. "Me neither, unless it's an emergency."

Aya nodded slowly but didn't say anything, just grabbed her tote and threw it over her shoulder. Kathleen nodded and turned back to her bed, straightening the comforter and throwing her clothes in the closet. She shoved her suitcase under the bed as a bell tolled over the loudspeaker— the signal that dinner was served. Alison turned her face back at the dresser, where the streams of the egg's energy burst from the crack. There was something about it that made her want to stay, but if she didn't show up for dinner the first night it would raise suspicions.

"All right, ladies." Kathleen smiled. "Are we ready for our first dinner here at the school?"

"Hell, yeah. I'm starving," Izzie grumped.

The rest of the girls nodded and waited for Kathleen to lead. Alison brought up the rear yet again.

9

fter the girls walked through the dining hall doors, they stopped and looked out over the vast sea of students. They could tell the upperclassman easily from the others. They sat at their tables with serious looks on their faces and whispered to each other as they scanned the fresh meat. Izzie hated it, it felt like she was trapped in some soap opera. She just wanted to get to her schooling, knowing how important a scholarship really was. Alison scanned the crowd too, but instead of looking for age she was looking for comforting energies. There were some, but the rest were mixed, some with envy, some pride, and others were too fast for her to really pinpoint.

"Well, come on, girls! Find a seat." The headmistress pushed them forward, motioning into the dining room.

The tables each sat seven people and were almost all full. There was an empty table next to the seniors, but before they could even set foot in that direction Wyatt and his friend sat down. They looked at the girls and snickered, then returned their attention to each other. Emma looked to her right, finding a table in the corner. She tapped Kathleen on the shoulder and motioned to it.

"I guess I can't be the center of attention *all* the time," Kathleen griped and, walking swiftly to the table, waited for the other girls to sit down.

Izzie sat next to Alison, smiling sweetly as she looked around the room. The whole place felt awkward; everyone searching for their places and finding their cliques. At the front of the hall was a stage with six round tables whose seats were filled with teachers. Izzie recognized a couple of them since she'd been there for several days. As her eyes slid from teacher to teacher she met Ms. Berens' stare. The headmistress nodded and then stood, pulling out her wand and waving it high in the air.

Orbs of light shot from the wand and spread out over the crowd. None of the upperclassmen seemed to notice since they were all used to the act, but the younger kids stared as the orbs reached their tables. The ball of energy danced around the table, creating a dish for each person. The glow of magic outlined Alison's food perfectly and gave her enough information to know what she was eating. In the center of each table were a large bowl of salad, different dressings, a plate of steaming-hot rolls, and a chocolate cake. In front of each student was the main course of chicken breasts in a berry sauce, asparagus, and potatoes au gratin. Kathleen smiled and nodded in approval.

"At least I know I'll eat healthy while I'm here. I've heard if you aren't careful you can gain a bunch of weight."

Emma looked down at her plate and at the chocolate

cake, sighing as she stabbed a piece of asparagus. As she raised the vegetable to her mouth she paused; Peter and Ethan were pulling out the empty chairs. They looked a bit less grungy than they had earlier, although Peter still had a stick tangled in his hair. Ethan gave the girls a big grin.

"Seats taken?"

Alison didn't even attempt to respond; they were partners in crime, since they knew about the egg. It seemed Kathleen felt the same way because all she did was scrunch her nose and shake her head. Ethan plopped into the chair next to her and looked at her food.

"Looks yum."

"If you would have been on time you would have known that from the beginning." Slowly Ethan turned around in his chair to find Ms. Berens standing over him with a raised eyebrow. "I'll excuse you this time, but next time you feast on bread and salad."

"Thank you." Peter grinned and stuck his wand in his pocket.

Ms. Berens sighed, rolled her eyes, swiped her wand, making two more plates of food appear. Peter grabbed his fork and started shoveling food in. Kathleen grimaced and turned to the side.

"Careful, you'll get your dribble on my plate."

Ms. Berens chuckled. "Boys will be boys, I suppose."

Ethan elbowed Peter and shook his head. Peter wrinkled his forehead but sat up straight and slowed down slightly. Alison thought it was funny but held her giggle back until Ms. Berens had gone back to her table. Everyone ate their dinners, their conversations growing louder as the comfort level grew. When they were done with the salad and main course, their plates disappeared, and cake plates appeared. A silver spatula floated over the dessert, cutting slices and depositing one on each saucer.

Alison laughed. Peter had chocolate icing smeared across his cheek. She turned to say something to Izzie, but the girl was staring across the room. She followed her gaze; the upperclassmen were quietly trying out different spells. The energy dissipated and reappeared each time a teacher looked over and then away.

They quietly waved their wands under the tables and small frogs jumped from the ends and hopped toward the lowerclassmen's tables. The boys laughed, trying to stomp the frogs, while the girls covered their mouths so as not to scream. A paper monkey swung wildly from the rafters above and Scarlett laughed as she moved her wand back and forth. The monkey stopped over a table of lowerclassmen and began to throw what looked like paper feces.

Ms. Berens looked up when she heard the girls scream and saw them dodging the paper poop and covering their plates. She shook her head and stood up, sending a bolt of energy from her hands to catch the monkey, which slowly turned to ash. She shot an angry glance toward Scarlett, who just shrugged and high-fived one of the girls at the table. Scarlett wasn't going to give up her persona just because she might land in detention. If anything, that would help her keep it.

"I can't wait to be an upperclassman." Kathleen had watched in wonder and now passed her cake to Peter. Emma, her fork halfway to her mouth, stopped and sighed, putting it down on her plate and waving it away. The plate disappeared, and a glass of water popped up in its place.

"So you can be an asshole to the younger kids?" Alison took a bite of her cake and Kathleen's energy sparked with just a tiny bit of red.

"It's a rite of passage, Alison. We all go through it and then deal it out. That's how it works. No one will respect us if we can't take a bit of harmless magic."

Ethan grimaced. "And what about harm*ful* magic, like the two guys who chased us through the woods sending orbs at us? They could have seriously hurt someone."

"All part of the game." Kathleen ignored Ethan's glare. "We'll go through it, our kids will go through it, and so on and so on."

Aya stared down at her plate as she listened to everyone talk and mumbled to herself, "Great. Hopefully my kids won't be shy like me."

Kathleen looked at her with pity. "That will wear off. You just have to get comfortable with your surroundings, that's all."

When everyone was done with their cake the teachers dismissed them. They had just enough time to get back to the dorms before curfew started and there was class the next day, so no one questioned going to bed. The girls changed into their pajamas and climbed under their covers, the beds instantly adjusting to whatever their comfort entailed. Alison was the last one to turn off her bedside lamp, leaving only the moonlight shining through the window to light the room. She stared out the window at the magical protection spells for the mansion swirling around the glass. The stars had their own energy; giant balls of gas and leftover magic from a long time before.

"*Psst,*" a voice hissed behind her. Alison turned over in the bed to face Emma.

"What's up?"

"Do you think classes will be hard?"

"I honestly don't know *what* to expect." Alison could see the nerves in Emma's energy. "But I am sure that whatever it is, you got it in the bag. You're gifted, and this is all about learning. They wouldn't just throw you to the wolves."

Emma lifted an eyebrow.

"I guess I should have phrased that better." Alison grimaced, thinking about the shifters. "You know what I mean."

"I know." Alison could hear the giggle in her voice. "I always get nervous for no reason, but I hate it. I get so worked up I don't notice how awesome a time I am having until after it's over."

"I'll be there with you, along with the rest of these girls. Just remember to breathe, and if you have questions don't be afraid to ask."

"Thanks, Alison."

"No problem, girl. Just get some sleep."

Alison wasn't sure where she had gotten the ability to give pep talks, but it had flowed out of her pretty easily. She had always been a sucker for someone in need, though, and Emma's energy had looked like she was about to burst from anxiety. Alison laid there watching Emma's energy until it calmed to a light blue, which told Alison that she was asleep. She turned back to the window and watched the swirls of energy from the stars to try to relax.

Her life was so different now. It was still challenging to grasp. She missed her mom and wondered what she would have told her about her first day here at the school. She just wanted to be normal; to have normal parents and worry less, like Kathleen. But that wasn't her life now and she was going to have to start getting used to it or she would never get into the swing of things.

As Alison sat at the window, her thoughts slowly faded, and she fell into a deep dreamless sleep. The next morning, she woke before the alarm went off. She slowly opened her eyes to see beams of sunlight swirling in oranges and reds. Though she had fallen asleep nervous, she awoke with excitement bubbling inside of her—and it seemed she wasn't the only one. Emma and Kathleen were already awake. Emma was sitting on the edge of her bed full of nervous energy as she stared down at the floor, while Kathleen was doing her makeup in the mirror.

The smell of breakfast was already wafting through the halls and Alison slowly sat up, stretching her arms high over her head. Her stomach rumbled loudly and she chuckled, rubbing it with her hand. She pulled herself from the comfortable mattress and straightened the sheets and comforter. Kathleen looked at her in the mirror.

"Use magic. Gets it perfect." She flicked her wand over her shoulder and the sheets folded over and pulled tight and the comforter raced up without a bump or wrinkle.

"I wish I could."

"Oh yeah. Sorry." Kathleen flicked her wand and Alison's bed was suddenly perfect. "There you go. I made it for you"

Alison giggled, putting out her hand for her shower bag as Kathleen slid it over just enough where she would find it, and walked out of the room toward the bathrooms.

None of the other girls were up yet, so she was able to shower and get back to the room before the others piled in. She put her bag down on the bed and slowly opened the top drawer, just making sure the egg was still in its place. It was still wrapped in her socks, energy whirling around it and the gold specks sparkling even brighter than before. She pushed in the drawer again and nabbed her bookbag to head off to breakfast.

First day of your new life. You can do this.

10

Eleanor Hudson took a deep breath, listening to the chatter outside the classroom. The first day of class was always invigorating for her. There were fresh minds just waiting to be filled. *She* knew, even if they didn't, that Basic Spells and History was one of the most important classes they would ever take. There were so many magical beings who were never taught the basics and the history behind it all. They were the ones who ended up with a Fixer pounding on their door, if not worse. Everything the students would learn from there on out would be based on her class, which made her proud.

While Mrs. Hudson finished preparing for her first class the girls sat in the dining hall, enjoying omelets made specifically to their individual specification. Kathleen's was spinach and so was Emma's, though hers had started as an extra-cheese omelet. Aya ate a mushroom, pepper, and cheese one, and Izzie had scrambled eggs instead. Alison wasn't sure if hers was an omelet or just scrambled, but it was the best breakfast she'd ever had.

"I need to learn how to make food like this with magic."

Kathleen smiled. "This is how my mother cooks, so it tastes just like home."

With that, the plates disappeared and Peter groaned, still chewing a mouthful. The bell tolled over the speaker, letting them know it was time to get to class. The girls all walked together, skirting a group of upperclassmen who were torturing the younger kids as they passed. Once past them they got in line. A smiling Mrs. Hudson stood at the door handing each student a textbook, looking at each of them through her thick, black-rimmed glasses.

"Good morning, Alison."

"Good morning, Mrs. Hudson."

"Here is your text." She leaned in, tapping it with her wand. "You will find the words easy to read with your Braille reader." She gave Alison a nudge and sent her into the room.

The classroom was large and the ceiling, taller than it had appeared from outside, showed bright blue skies and two moons in the distance, just like Oriceran would look. Alison sat at a desk in the second row and Izzie took a seat on one side and Peter the other. Mrs. Hudson swished her wand to close the doors and made her way to the front. She stood there for a moment looking at all the fresh faces, confident in her favorite black power suit and heels. She clapped her hands to get the attention of the entire class.

"Welcome to your first class at the School of Necessary Magic. I will be your instructor for Basic Spells and

History. For those who haven't yet met me, my name is Mrs. Hudson."

Eleanor waved her wand at the chalkboard and her name appeared in cursive.

"I have just a few rules for the first day. One, no wands or magic will be needed; we will be diving into the history of Oriceran. Two, if you have a question please raise your hand. No question is a stupid question, and every one of you should remember that. Three, take notes, especially on the history part. There will be a test and a final exam."

As she spoke, her words appeared on the board behind her. Emma turned and glanced at Alison, giving her a reassuring pat. Mrs. Hudson put her wand in the inner pocket of her jacket.

"Now open your texts to the first chapter. We'll start with the Great Treaty."

The rustle of pages filled the classroom as each student quietly opened their book and flipped to the first chapter. There was an artist's depiction of Oriceran on the first page, the Light Elf mansion high in the sky and green grasses flowing through the fields. Izzie blinked and the magic in the book swirled until it created the scene for her. She smiled and looked up at Mrs. Hudson, who nodded and looked away.

"To my knowledge, all of you know at least something about Oriceran, and others of you have even been there. Today's lesson goes back sixteen thousand years to a time where war raged on Oriceran. For centuries they looked for peace, but none could be found. Finally, different creatures from across Oriceran came together to create one of the most important documents in their history, the Great

Treaty. The Great Treaty set up rules and understandings about the portals between Earth and Oriceran and how they open, but only during certain periods. The rest of the time travel between the worlds was forbidden without the express permission of the Council."

The students read along in the chapter, looking at different pictures and the rules spelled out by the treaty.

"When the portal to Earth first opened many magical beings came to Earth and some humans went to Oriceran. When the portal was closing many of those beings decided to stay here, which is where most of you came from. The treaty has been in effect for sixteen thousand-plus years, but recently it has been threatened more than once. Can anyone tell me one instance?"

She looked at several students who had their hands up.

"Yes, Kathleen?"

"When I visited last, I overheard my mother talking about some sort of artifact race."

"Yes," Eleanor replied, tapping the table to her right. "Exactly. Magical beings generally live much longer than humans, and we have powers on Oriceran that aren't as strong when we're here. That is where the kemanas and the artifacts come into play. For this class we will be talking about artifacts. These trinkets, some completely random like spoons, sundials, lamps, or even clothing, are given stores of energy—magic, if you will. When a magical being needs a boost on Earth, they can basically use these artifacts to recharge. Now, before I get into the artifact race, it's important to understand how all this got started."

Eleanor used her wand to erase the rules and turned back toward the class, clasping her hands in front of her.

"There is a seer—a woman who can tell the future—and she has foretold that the next time the portal opens Oriceran will lose all its power and cease to exist. That means magical beings will have to migrate to this planet and set up shop here on Earth. The prophecy is not written in stone, but many are basing their futures on that prediction. Because of that, magic has started to become more visible to the people of Earth, giving them a chance to ease into lives next to magical beings. Some are scared and others curious, but where change comes, so do those looking to profit. That is where the race for artifacts comes into play."

Emma put her hand in the air and Eleanor nodded.

"Don't the Silver Griffins have a vault they store artifacts in?"

"They do." Mrs. Hudson smiled, nodding. "It used to be in Chicago, but that one was destroyed. The new location isn't known and they don't have all the artifacts, either. So many of them are hidden here on Earth, and will be very difficult to find. The large corporations, both Oriceran and human-run, think that if they own powerful artifacts they will be able to stay in power once our worlds collide. So— as you can imagine, having been around humans a lot in your lives—they are doing whatever they can to collect artifacts. Yes, Aya?"

"Aren't most artifacts dangerous for humans?"

"Good question, but the answer is a bit vague. It seems some humans are capable of using the artifacts to open portals to Oriceran, and others who pay no attention to the energy in these pieces end up a mist of flesh and bone."

"I don't think it's right that they take what isn't theirs," Ethan yelled.

"And I would agree with you," Eleanor responded. "Unfortunately, we brought them here—or created them here—and therefore they have as much say as we do. They experiment with artifacts to create a new version of this world. In short, yes, it is unfair, but we were the ones who enabled them."

Eleanor talked about the wars, the prophecy, and what they were doing to help prevent problems during the first part of the class.

"We have been working with the government and some for-hire mercenaries to make the transition for everyone just a bit easier. Even our headmistress has someone on the inside, working diligently to keep order and pave our way to interact smoothly with the humans around us. It is the first time in our history on Earth that we are pushing to use magic around humans."

Alison listened carefully, shocked to find out that magical beings were on the verge of becoming one with the community around them. She was a bit skeptical though, having spent her fair share of time around humans and never seeing much more than greed and pride. She didn't dislike them, but she knew they weren't educated on magic and thus feared it. It was all about power, and with a power struggle usually comes an ugly battle.

"I'd like the class to take the next ten minutes to read through the bullet points of the treaty. When you are done we will all switch and have a little fun doing some basic spellcasting."

The class cheered and Mrs. Hudson laughed, then

erased the words from the board. She sat down at her desk and flipped through her lesson plan, making sure she had verbally touched on the most important parts. The details they could study on their own. They were only allotted a certain amount of time per class, and there was a lot to cover with the first-years.

When the ten minutes were up and the last of the students had finished reading, Mrs. Hudson stood at the front of the class. She waved her wand in a circle and produced a small orb of light, then put out her palm and bounced the orb up and down. She finally tossed it at Ethan, who had dozed off. It hit him in the nose with a shower of sparks and he woke up, swatting at the sparks that rolled over his desk.

The class laughed as he panicked before looking up at Mrs. Hudson with a sheepish grin. She shook her head, unable to hold back a smirk, and did the spell again, this time saying the incantation aloud.

"*Fizzing Bulb*," she chanted, swishing her wand.

The light raced around the room and back to her palm, where it disappeared in a puff of smoke.

"All right, class, groups of eight and try the spell with each other."

11

The girls plus Peter, and Ethan formed their group. They looked around the classroom and the others had done the same, navigating toward those they had met during the first day. They were all excited to try the new spells—and spells in general—though Kathleen couldn't help but scoff at the simplicity of their practice spell.

"I guess everyone has to start somewhere, right?"

"Very true, Kathleen." Mrs. Hudson had walked up behind her, catching Kathleen off-guard.

"Mrs. Hudson, I just meant that some of us are past orb creation, that's all."

"Well, then, this should be a breeze for you." She smiled and pulled a tall blond headed boy up next to her. He looked nervous, but there was something kind behind his eyes. "I would like you all to meet Luke, who is without a group. He will be observing so he can understand the technique for the finals and beyond."

"You aren't doing magic?" Emma tilted her head to the side.

Alison already knew he wouldn't be, since she could read it in his soul. His cheeks grew a bit red and he looked down, scuffing his shoe against the floor. Mrs. Hudson cleared her throat.

"Luke here is a shifter, so no, he won't be doing any spellcasting."

Everyone slowly nodded and she walked away. They opened their circle enough for Luke to join, but none of them said anything to him. Shifters tended to be stronger and faster than most, and because they lacked the ability to do actual spells they put their energies into sports. Luke was no exception, and the group shied away from him.

In both the magical community on Earth and on Oriceran, shifters were thought of as second-tier magical beings. Most of them started out as ordinary human beings and were turned into shifters by some sort of dark magic, but there was no going back once the creation was complete—and once they carried that gene, their children, grandchildren, and those down the line also ran the risk of becoming shifters. Luke had been born that way, another jock in a long line of wolf-shifters.

These creatures could be very helpful, since their animal was usually strong-willed, vicious when needed, and able to withstand strong magical blows. But because they held only the ability to shift, they were shunned. It also didn't help that when they shifted they became massive scary wolves, which frightened the magical and non-magical alike. That was how the human tales of the werewolves had begun, the biggest difference being that typical shifters didn't hunt human prey—and most of them were pretty decent when one got to know them.

Kathleen stepped forward and cleared her throat, causing Ethan to roll his eyes. "Let me go first." Ethan stepped in front of Kathleen, smirking at her. "You can't always be the superstar."

"Fine, whatever."

Ethan decided to use his wizard side, not wanting a glow from his elf half if it could be avoided. He swirled his wand for a moment to gather energy and pointed his wand at his palm, creating a small orb. He bounced it around in his hand for a moment then sent it out, focusing his intention on Kathleen, who wasn't paying attention.

The orb hit her face with a crackle and hiss and she grabbed her nose, glaring at Ethan. When she pulled her hand away the tip was sooty from the orb. She narrowed her eyes and growled, stepping up and swirling her wand to create an even bigger orb. The smile faded from Ethan's face and he stepped back, putting his hands up.

"It was just a joke."

"It *hurt*," she ground out.

Kathleen took another step forward and sent the orb spiraling at his face. Right before it hit him, Luke caught the orb bare-handed and crushed it to dust. Kathleen gaped as the dust settled into a pile at Luke's feet. The shifter took a step back and nodded at Ethan, but Ethan shook his head and brought him in for a pat on the back.

"Thanks, man. She just about took my head off my shoulders."

"Whatever..." Kathleen rolled her eyes, flinching as Mrs.

Hudson walked up behind her and put her hands on her shoulders.

"Let's make sure we keep the orbs small, yes?"

"Sorry."

The girls took turns creating small orbs and sending them spiraling at the guys, including Luke. They weren't fond of him, but they could tell he was used to that reaction and none of them wanted to purposely make him feel bad.

When it was Alison's turn, she was nervous stepping into the center of the circle and pulling the energy into her palm. She was able to pull a small amount of energy but couldn't form an orb, and after a few minutes, she stepped back. She didn't feel bad, though. At least she had accomplished *something*.

Ethan stepped up and rolled up his sleeves, ready to do it again, only this time they would all get a taste of their own medicine. He created a small orb and sent it out, nipping Kathleen in the cheek. The orb didn't dissipate this time, but it skipped to the next person, then the next until finally everyone except Alison had tasted Ethan's wrath. They were laughing hysterically. When he was done he stepped back, giving the floor back to Kathleen. She looked at Peter, who was digging in his pockets, and gave him a glare.

"All right, all right, make the circle tighter," Peter whispered to the group, not wanting Mrs. Hudson to overhear. "I've been working with science and magic since I was a little kid and I can cast this cool spell."

Kathleen raised both eyebrows in irritation. "And?"

Peter smiled and pulled out a vial of aluminum flash

powder, which he dumped in one palm. He clasped his wand tightly in his other hand and pulled an orb, letting it roll around in the powder, then whispered something under his breath too quietly for anyone to hear and held his palm out flat. The orb morphed into a tiny Gnome, who broke off chunks of energy and pelted everyone in the circle with it. The Gnome chuckled and disappeared into thin air, leaving a group of stunned magical kids.

"That was awesome," Ethan gasped. "Do it again."

"All right, but you better tell me if the teacher looks over here."

Peter did the spell again, this time holding the Gnome for a lot longer. The little beast threw tiny balls of light around the room, zapping every one of his classmates. When Mrs. Hudson turned around to see what all the ruckus was about he slammed his hands together, extinguishing the energy before it got him in trouble. He loved working with science and magic; to him there was nothing better, although others thought it was risky and dangerous.

Mrs. Hudson gave the group a knowing stare. She was sure they were doing something sneaky, but she hadn't been quite fast enough to catch them in the act. Peter backed out of the middle of the group and stood next to Alison, trying to hold back his laughter. Alison liked Peter; he had an awesome soul, he didn't take himself too seriously, and he wasn't afraid to try something even if imminent death or a very painful mistake would be the result. Alison couldn't help but admit that he was pretty talented. She was impressed and was glad he was on his way to becoming one of her closest friends at the school.

Max Regency only stood about three feet tall, but he made up for his lack of stature with his demeanor and snazzy dress. He was a Gnome; one with some seriously strong talents. He walked to the front of the class in a white button-up, suspenders, tie, dress pants, and a pair of boots. In his right hand he held a glass of whiskey, the same one he had filled early that morning. Everyone thought he drank because he was so deep in thought, but in reality, he barely imbibed any of the liquid he carried around all day. *Gotta make up for being a Gnome by being a badass magician.*

Max was the Channeling Energy teacher, a skill that came in especially handy for elves. They pulled their energy from the ground, and from those around them. The class was a way for the witches and wizards to learn something new about doing magic without the use of a wand. He stood and looked at the students, thankful he had an audience for once. He had spent half the class time talking about philosophy, but finally got to the real deal—he helped each person channel their energy, control it, and send it back out again.

Several of the witches gave it a shot, half envious of the elves and the other half seeing them as a threat to their powers. Either way, everyone but Luke was given a chance to show how well they could channel their energy. Alison had a special advantage, she was completely in touch with the energy around her, since she used streams of energy to compensate for her lack of sight. She had never tried what he was talking about, but she knew it was the key to gaining control over her magic. Just knowing that, and knowing how close she was to it, she got cocky.

"Very good, Ethan." Max patted Ethan on the shoulder. "All right, who's left?"

Ethan stumbled back to his seat and sat down hard due to the exhaustion channeling brought. At the same time, he realized how much more he could do if he were able to calm his emotions rather than let them get the best of him and his magic. The others nodded in approval at Ethan, which made him proud. Max scanned the class and stopped at Alison.

"Alison, we haven't seen anything from you yet."

Alison nodded and stood up, breathing heavily with nerves. As she walked past Emma, the girl reached out and grabbed her arm, squeezing it to remind her not to be nervous. Alison let out the breath she was holding and made her way to the front of the room.

When she reached the front Max stared at her for a moment. He saw something he hadn't seen before, but he couldn't put his finger on it. This girl was powerful, he could tell, but he could also tell that she had no idea what she was capable of. He wanted to ease her into the channeling since it was in her best interest, but before he could she was already knee-deep and there was nothing he could do to stop it. The magic flowed through her, unlike anything any of them had seen before.

Alison wanted to impress her new friends. She wanted them to see that she was more than just a brave girl with no tricks. She had been through so much, and the rush of impressing these people would be what she needed to start moving forward. What Alison didn't realize was just how hard it would be to control the energy.

She stepped up, as Max Regency cautiously stared at her. She could see the souls of all the students in front of her, her friends' souls being the most familiar. There was an air of curiosity in the wavering energy around each person. None of them knew what to expect from the pretty little silver-tipped girl at the front of the class.

Before Max could give her instructions, she closed her eyes and focused. Her arms and fingers tingled, and waves of warmth rushed up her legs and through her veins, gathering in her belly. She just felt warm, but she was putting on a display of magic that left her classmates speechless.

Bright rays of light burst from her belly, and she looked like a star on its way to death.

As the energy grew stronger, the other students put their arms up in front of their eyes to shield them from the light. Alison had never felt her powers before, but it was like they were guiding her at every step. She wanted to release the energy, but she didn't know how. *Show me,* her voice whispered in her mind, and while outside there was a storm, inside she was calm and collected.

The next feeling started as a tingle in the tip of her finger and began to move down her arm and across her chest. She waited for it, feeling it, knowing it would lead her to the next step. As it touched her stomach she could feel the energy trying to force its way outward. She let out a deep breath of air and released, pushing her shoulders backward and her stomach out. She lifted so high on her toes that only the tips touched the floor.

Max yelled her name as light burst from her stomach and swirled around the classroom. The students gripped their desks as the metal legs scraped across the floors and the room began to spin, slowly at first, but picking up speed. Books flew off shelves and pictures crashed to the floor in a massive pile of broken glass. When Max reached up and grabbed her arm to rein her back in, he could feel the energy flowing through her.

When Alison released the energy, the weight lifted from her chest and air returned to her lungs. All she could focus on was the magic; everything else was just background noise. She could hear Mr. Regency call her name, but she couldn't focus enough to respond. Suddenly a hand clamped down on her arm and pulled her back to the ground. She opened her eyes wide, following the light swirling from her body and racing around the classroom. "You flipped the classroom completely around," gasped a student.

"How do I fix this!?" She was afraid and had no idea what to do next.

"Just follow my voice with your energy around the room. Don't move too fast or too slow, just follow the voice."

Alison shook her head and closed her eyes again, still feeling the magic bursting from her. Mr. Regency spoke quickly but firmly, leading her energy around the room counterclockwise. Slowly the room began to turn, everything in it making its way back to the correct position. He was grounding her; showing her that her magic could be controlled.

"Okay, it's back in place. All you have to do now is stop the energy. You channeled it, now let it go." Max kept a firm hand on her arm.

Alison took in a deep breath and pulled the magic back, forcing it down her body, and back into the ground beneath her feet. Suddenly there was silence. Alison opened her eyes and stared at the souls of the shocked students, who were sitting perfectly still. Their energy was vibrating rapidly, shimmering in deep colors.

After a few more moments of awkward silence, Kathleen stood up and threw her arms in the air.

"That was awesome!"

The class erupted into cheers, filling Alison's heart with affection. Kathleen knew full well that it hadn't been awesome. It had been dangerous as hell to be out on a limb like that with the teacher at a loss for words, but that didn't stop her from being there for Alison. When the cheers had quieted Alison turned toward the Gnome, feeling a little more than light-headed, then stumbled backward and grabbed the desk. Max walked toward her, putting out his hand.

"Are you all right?"

"I feel… Just tired." Alison's eyes rolled back and she began to fall forward as Peter ran up and dropped to his knees, catching her before she hit the ground. He quickly turned her over on her back and looked down at her face, completely calm. Mr. Regency checked her vitals, which were all normal, and looked at Peter.

"Give her a moment. She will come back to consciousness on her own."

After a few minutes, Alison moaned. Her classmates still sat silently, waiting and hoping that she would be okay. Alison opened her eyes and looked up at Peter, and then at her teacher. She sat up slowly and rubbed her head, unsure what had just happened.

"Take your time." Peter smiled down at her.

The bell rang and everyone got up slowly and made their way out of the room, but Alison still sat there trying to get her head to clear. She had done something she hadn't even known she was capable of, but now she was left with the magical hangover.

***

Kathleen, Izzie, Emma, and Aya whispered to each other in the library, worried about whether Alison was alright.

Classes were over for the day and they were there study-ing, waiting to see Alison. They wanted to see if everything that happened was normal for whatever type of magical being she was. It was a bit hard to take, considering the first time she did magic she had spun their classroom around and then fainted.

Ethan walked into the library and looked for the girls, then worked his way through the room and sat down at their table. He pulled out his notebook and leaned his head on his hand, trying to stay hidden when he talked. He knew Gnomes didn't play games and the librarian wasn't going to let them get away with chatting it up in study hall.

"They sent me out," he whispered. "I don't know if she is okay."

Someone cleared their throat next to Ethan and he slowly looked over, coming face to face with Leo. Ethan plastered a huge smile on his face and looked down at his book, pretending to study. Leo cleared his throat again.

"No talking in here."

"Yes, sir," Ethan replied, making the zipper gesture across his lips. "Lips sealed."

Just then Peter walked through the door of the library with Alison. She looked much better than she had when they'd left her in the classroom; the color was starting to come back to her cheeks. The girls stayed silent, waving for her and Peter to join their group. Leo Decker narrowed his eyes, his red poppy still blowing raspberries. He could sense the power in her, which was greater than most of the magical beings in the school. At the same time, he under-stood she had no idea what kind of power she had inside her, or how to use it.

Izzie pulled out the chair beside her and Alison smiled, sitting down and putting her books in front of her. She glanced at the other girls, who gave her sympathetic glances. Behind her she could hear whispering, and she could see Scarlett's familiar energy out of the corner of her eye. She did the best to ignore them, but when Scarlett tapped her on the shoulder she had no choice but to turn around.

"We heard you tried to blow up the channeling room." Scarlett smirked.

Alison rolled her eyes and turned back around, grabbing a pencil and sticking the end between her teeth. She knew it wouldn't be the end of it, but she really hoped Scarlett would take a hint. It was obviously too much to hope for; Scarlett leaned toward their table.

"I mean, we're fine with that, it's a stupid class anyway, but shit, those are your friends. Are you psycho?"

Ethan put his arm between the girls, resting it nonchalantly on the back of Alison's chair, then slowly turned his head and stared at Scarlett. She looked him up and down and chuckled for a moment.

"Leave her alone."

"Oh, big scary street urchin." Scarlett and her friends laughed nastily.

Alison reached out till she felt his chest to get his attention. "Don't. They aren't worth it."

Ethan nodded, understanding that fighting fire with fire never really worked. He turned back and looked at Peter, who was fiddling with the pencil. Ethan could tell he needed to calm down, so he leaned forward.

"You should do one of those orb spells and hit these

girls right in the foreheads."

"Ha!" Peter laughed. "Not if I want to keep my thumbs. The librarian here will kick my ass. It's all quiet all the time for him."

"All right, then help me with my homework."

"That I can do."

Peter scooted closer to Ethan and looked down at the paper, pointing to different sections in his book. Alison smiled and nodded at Ethan, knowing he was taking Peter's mind off what had just happened. It had freaked everyone out, there was no doubt about that, but they still wanted to be Alison's friend. She just wanted to get back to her regular agenda. Starting her first day by flipping a classroom hadn't been on her agenda.

When the group was done with study hall, they headed down to get some dinner. As they walked in the whole place got quiet and everyone's eyes followed Alison to her seat. Slowly the whispers and talking picked up again and Alison was glad to know they were nice enough to move on and not harass her like the upperclassman were doing.

Ms. Berens looked at Alison from the front of the dining hall and nodded to herself, having already heard of the trouble she'd had in channeling class. The girl needed some major training, major control, and major guidance, and she needed it as soon as possible.

Alison just hoped that she would get a good night's sleep and that her friends wouldn't force her to talk about it. She had tapped into magical energy—a magic she didn't know she had—but she had to figure out how to use it before something happened that was worse than a reversed classroom.

13

Time went by, and the further Alison got into the teachings the more she could feel the desire of her magic. It was like having another person inside her body and her mind. She tossed and turned at night from nightmares of the night her mother died, and by day her energy burst at the seams. By the time the alarm went off—which was before the sun came up—she was already awake.

The girls had all started getting up earlier, wanting to make it to breakfast to have enough time to eat before their plates disappeared and the bell tolled. That morning Izzie woke up to Kathleen slapping the alarm clock and mumbling something about omelets. She climbed out of bed, grabbed her things, and headed off to the showers. When she came back the other girls were doing the same. Alison, who was completely ready, was sitting on the edge of her bed and staring at the floor. Izzie walked over and sat down next to her.

"Nightmares again?"

"Yeah." Alison rubbed her face quickly. "I didn't wake you up, did I?"

"Nah, you were quiet all night. I guess I'm a morning person."

"I've never been a morning person." Alison cracked a smile, which relieved Izzie.

"Hey, you want to head down to breakfast? The slow-pokes can catch up."

"Sounds perfect."

Alison and Izzie walked out of the room, saying hi to some of the other girls before leaving the dorms behind them and heading down to the dining hall. It had been a while since everything had happened with Alison, and everyone had all but forgotten about it. When they got to the hall they headed straight to their table, sitting down and staring down at the plates that appeared in front of them. Izzie had a cheese omelet like normal, but Alison had a stack of pancakes—something different for a change.

The girls sat quietly, enjoying their breakfast and drinking coffee as their classmates started to trickle in. Izzie looked around the large room, realizing it was the first time she had taken a moment to appreciate the grandiose nature of the place. They were always so busy. When they weren't jetting off to class or trying to cram in homework, they were interacting with the group. It was nice to have a little bit of quiet for a change.

The large and ornate room was beautiful. It had been Turner Underwood's ballroom many years before when he lived there. The ceiling curved up into a dome, its panels etched with the different magical creatures from Oriceran.

In the center hung the massive crystal chandelier with hundreds of candles in black steel holders. All the oval tables were made of a rich dark mahogany and the chairs were high-backed, their upholstery stitched with shining brown, maroon, and golden thread. Every person who ate in the dining hall felt like a king or a queen.

The enchanted sky in the dome changed depending on the time of day and the weather outside. On rainy days it would show a sunny day inside, running the rain late at night to let the students enjoy a relaxing evening. It rarely ever stormed from the ceiling, which kept the mood light and upbeat regardless of what was going on in the outside world. Everything in the dining hall was elegant and rich, right down to the appearing and disappearing dishes on the tables.

Izzie couldn't ever remember seeing anything like this mansion before. Even though her mind was always fuzzy, she did have bits and pieces of memories from the orphanage. That place, from what she could remember, was dank and dirty, its funds low but its expectations high. She didn't fully understand why she didn't have more memories of her childhood, but she figured they probably wouldn't have mattered anyway.

"You guys went off without us." Kathleen pulled out her chair and a plate full of fruit appeared before her.

"Yeah, we were hungry and ready, so we bolted over here." Alison took another bite of pancakes and Kathleen looked at her banana and then back at Alison's pancakes, then changed her order mid-meal.

As the crowds began to pour into the dining hall, the normal excited chatter filled the air. Izzie smiled to herself, then sighed. She had really enjoyed the quiet time, but she was glad to know she had friends on her side. It was the last thing she had expected when she had woken up at the school, and to know that she was creating a family for herself made her feel really positive about her future. She was living in a beautiful mansion, had people around her who never hounded her for her secrets, and was learning magic for the first time. Still, somewhere in the pit of her stomach was something unsaid; something missing that churned and scraped to get out. She didn't know what it was, but eventually she would have to give in.

As if the headmistress could read her mind, she walked over and put her hand on Izzie's shoulder. Izzie looked up at her, wondering what she had come over there for. Kathleen swallowed a bite of her pancakes, rolling her eyes in pleasure before she noticed Ms. Berens standing there staring at her.

"Oh. Sorry." Kathleen covered her full mouth and giggled.

"Carbs are good for you sometimes." The headmistress smiled. "How are you girls this morning?"

They all nodded. Izzie looked up and smiled. She wanted to ask questions about the orphanage, but she didn't want the other girls to know. She would just have to wait, and hopefully the blanks would start to fill in.

Elias Hodges stood in his perfectly-fitted tailor-made suit and white button-up shirt, writing on the chalkboard. His hair was dark brown and slicked back, his beard perfectly trimmed and maintained, and his eyes were chestnut with hints of gold. The girls thought he was dreamy and the guys got the creeps, seeing the wolf that hid under the surface.

Elias taught the Transfiguration class, and that day's lesson was about shifters. This was a subject Elias knew more about than he was willing to teach the students. He himself was a shifter, coming from a long line of wolves. His great-grandfather had been an Alpha. Elias didn't want to lead a pack. He wanted to teach others about the shifters, and he hoped that one day they could all live in harmony with one another. He was pragmatic, though. He knew that it took a lot more than classroom chat to make the students trust him.

"All right, guys, so today we are going to tackle the taboo and have an uncomfortable conversation about shifters. Shifters are interesting creatures. I know, because I am one. Some shifters are first-generation, meaning they were changed by dark magic. Others come from a long line of shifters, some even dating back to the first ones to set foot on Earth from Oriceran. Who here can tell me something about shifters?" Elias looked around the room at the one or two hands up. "Yes, Peter?"

"Shifters don't need a full moon to change like the human legends tell us."

"Very good. And that is true, we can change at any time, but most of us stick to dark nights so we don't cause a panic. Anyone else? Yes, Kathleen?"

"Shifters are extremely loyal creatures. They not only bond with their pack like a family, they will be there for those they care about no matter what."

"Yes, another great example. Shifters don't think of family the same way humans do. To shifters, a brother or sister may be someone they have never met until they get together with their pack. As far as helping others, we bond with people and vow to keep those people safe from harm, no matter what. Right, Luke?"

Several people shifted in their seats, glancing at Luke then back at the professor. Luke sank down in his chair, slightly uncomfortable with getting called out even if it was by another shifter. He had enough problems finding his place here, the last thing he needed was for people to think he and the teacher had some sort of strange bond. He just wanted to play sports and go on to college.

A few of the kids snickered and made fun of shifters, acting as if no one were paying attention. Ethan hated fake people like that. In his mind you either accepted or you let your fear turn you into an asshat, and that was what was happening to those kids. He pulled his wand out, swishing it underneath the table and sending jolts of lightning up their legs and into their stomach. The kids began to cough, rubbing their legs and moving up to their stomachs. They looked at Ethan angrily, but he didn't care. He was tired of assholes, and tired of magical creatures always being at war.

When the class was over Ethan headed out and the three boys he had jolted stopped him in the courtyard. The largest one and speaker for the group raised his dark hood over his head and pulled out his wand, poking Ethan in the chest with it.

"You think you are so smooth and cool, but you didn't

think about the repercussions. You can be a wolf-lover all you want, but they don't belong with us."

"That's unfortunate."

The kid growled and lifted his wand as black sparks shot from the end. Before he could release the magic Aya and Alison ran out to the courtyard. Alison started to pull energy while Aya lifted her wand and shot a small fireball, which knocked the boy to the side. He hit the ground hard and his wand bounced across the grass. She was pissed, and no longer able to sit back and watch as bullies picked on kids over and over again. Ethan and Alison glanced at each other and then looked at Aya in surprise.

"I'm not *always* a wimp."

Alison could feel her energy trying to get out, but after the stunt in class a week before she had made it a point to stay back from any kind of magic. Her mother had taught her some pretty badass fight moves though, and she was ready to take on the three fools in front of them. Alison ran forward with her fists up, concentrating on the shifting light from their souls. She swept her leg and knocked one of the boys off his feet. She leaned over him, blinking her eyes.

"You stay away from the shifters, get it? Otherwise, you will answer to me."

The boy nodded wildly as Alison stood up and backed away. The leader helped the boy up, and he spat blood onto the ground and growled. He nodded, turning the boys away and pushed them back into the school. Aya lowered her wand and Alison walked over.

"That was pretty sweet there."

Aya blushed and smiled. "Thanks. I hate bullies."

"Me too, girl. Me too."

They both slapped Ethan on the shoulder and walked back into the school. Ethan stood there for a second, unsure whether to be flattered, thankful, or pissed that someone else had fought his fight. In the end, though, he was just happy a point had been made.

14

"Did you see that guy's face?" Aya giggled quietly. "I think he might have shit himself."

"What happened?" Izzie leaned in, interested.

"Oh, nothing, just Aya kicking some magical ass." Alison laughed, although they were trying to stay quiet as they waited for their next teacher.

"And you kicking some *literal* tail." Aya put up her fists.

"Sorry I missed that!" Izzie chuckled, knowing there was probably nothing she could have done to help. No shoestrings to tie.

The bell rang to signal the beginning of class and everyone got quiet, looking around the room and wondering where the teacher was. The classroom was huge and there were large maps hung haphazardly all over the walls. Artifacts sat in big glass cases. Some moved and twitched behind their magical shields, while others looked completely innocuous. The whole place was a bit of a mess.

Which made Miss Grant's late entrance not all that unusual.

The doors slammed open and a woman with long brown hair, dress pants, flats, a white t-shirt, and a thick cardigan came tumbling through the doors. Papers slipped from the stack she was carrying and Peter jumped up, picked them up from the ground, and set them back on the stack in her arms. She sighed and nodded at Peter, taking off down the rows of chairs and setting the stack down on the desk at the front. She put her hand on top of the stack and looked up at the ceiling for a moment, mumbling something to herself. Alison could see the wild energy around her. She was a scatterbrained witch and seemed to have a million emotions and thoughts whizzing around her.

Finally, she looked back down, grabbed her wand, and swished it. A cabinet to the right, which was filled to the brim with textbooks, opened. Miss Grant looked down at the sheet of paper in front of her and slid her finger down the names.

"Peter and Ethan," she called. "Pass out textbooks, please. Kathleen, take these packets and pass them out. Thank you."

Kathleen shined, loving being called on for anything that let her display herself. She walked to the front of the class and took the pile of papers before following behind the boys. Everyone got a textbook and a packet, which looked more like a hodgepodge than school information.

"The words in my textbook are changing." One of the students held the book in the air.

"Yes. This is your Hidden Earth class, and since the

revelation of magic to the humans there have been constant changes to the rules and regulations sections. Just ignore it. We will fight through that section together when we get there. For now, focus on the history. No one can change that, not even us."

Miss Grant walked up and down the aisles as she waited for all the textbooks to be delivered. As she walked past Alison she tapped her book nonchalantly with her wand. The book came to life in Alison's hands, the spells working together to form text on the pages, outlined in magic. It seemed all the teachers were on the same page when it came to her inability to see the world normally.

"Why do the teachers keep tapping your textbooks?" Emma whispered.

Alison shrugged, playing it off, but Izzie could tell there was more to it than she was saying. She didn't press the issue though, seeing as how she had her own suitcase full of secrets and lies. When everyone had a textbook Miss Grant took in a deep breath and slowly let it out, then headed back to the front. She swirled her wand on the chalkboard, scribbling her name almost illegibly.

"I am Miss Annabelle Grant, and I am a witch and your Hidden Earth instructor. In this class we will discuss the kemanas—the underground worlds—and the railway system—the magical one. Some of you are very familiar with these things and others not so much, so let's be patient with each other and really delve in. The final will be based on what is going on at that time, so learn the basics of hidden earth and memorize it, but don't let any one event stick too tightly in your mind."

Aya leaned toward Alison to grumble, "Great class, where you aren't sure what you are supposed to learn."

Alison smiled and glanced at Izzie. Her energy told her Izzie was completely enthralled by her text. She had forgotten that not everyone had been through magic like she had. Some of them were almost brand-new to even the idea. The wonder they must be feeling, learning all about this magical world that no one had ever told them about; to realize all your childhood stories were true in some way or another. Alison was almost jealous of them and somewhere in the back of her mind she wished she could start over and feel that excitement and wonder again. To feel the mystical energy that surrounded the world of magic without it being tainted by darkness and death.

"We will start with kemanas." Miss Grant swished her wand and an orb of light glided over the students and hung in the center of the room, pulsing. A magical trail drew in the school above it. "A kemana is a power source, something that holds a massive amount of energy and slowly leaks it out on Earth. Usually it is some sort of stone or rock, but there have been times where a strong-enough magical being has put it in an artifact. Now, these kemanas are our recharging stations, if you will. Our magic wanes here on Earth and there are only three ways to renew that energy: artifacts, kemanas, or a trip to Oriceran."

The orb began to pulse faster and spat strands of white light that ran through the map of the school.

"The School of Necessary Magic was built on top of a kemana." Miss Grant continued. "This kemana in the ground beneath our feet keeps Izzie steady flow of magic our school needs at full capacity. It enhances all the magic on this property, so you may feel a difference in your magic here versus off the school grounds. It is not as strong as going to Oriceran, but it is enough for what we are doing here. There are kemanas scattered all over the Earth, protected by underground cities."

The page in the textbook turned and Izzie looked down at a diagram of a kemana and underground city. There were shops, magical beings, and even places to live. To the right was a train station, but it too was underground. Miss Grant glanced at one of her papers as it lifted into the air and caught fire, quickly burning to a pile of ash that floated down onto the desk. She sighed and shook her head.

"Another big move with magic." She turned back to the class and pursed her lips. "Who here has ever ridden a train or subway?"

Everyone in the class put their hands up.

"Good, now who here has ever ridden the magical underground train?"

Most of the hands went down, but Kathleen's, Peter's, and Ethan's hands stayed up. Izzie raised her eyebrow, unsure if she had ever been on one, but she assumed most likely not.

"Excellent. Now, for those of you who *didn't* know, a magical railway system connects all the kemanas. This country has its own, and the others do as well. You can be sure that wherever there is a kemana, there is an entrance to its underground city somewhere. You can also be sure that where there is a cluster of Starbucks, there will be an entry to the railway platform for that area."

"Why Starbucks?"

"Well, it wasn't always Starbucks, of course, but as time

has gone by we have found that there was a large enough diversity in clientele, and that they are always packed. Therefore, no one would notice people walking down the bathroom hall and disappearing into the magical wall. Most of the humans are oblivious anyway these days, too absorbed in coffee and technology to notice anything out of the ordinary."

Izzie put up her hand and Miss Grant nodded at her. "So anyone magical can just stand in a kemana and basically fill up?"

"Yep." Miss Grant giggled. "Like a magical gas station. Most of the time you will find a large number of magical folks in Earth communities near kemanas. We can feel their power, and because we don't want to run out of magic we stay close. The one under the school is cloaked from outsiders, though. We don't want this to be a Texaco for magical folks. All right, everyone stand up. We're going to do an exercise."

Izzie and Alison glanced at each other and slowly rose from their seats. The whole class stood behind their chairs waiting for the instructor to say something. She pulled out her wand and smiled.

"Do you feel anything?"

"No," Kathleen replied, looking around. Everyone else shook their heads.

"Because the buzz is cloaked. Now hold one second."

Miss Grant raised her wand and began to whisper an enchantment. She was so quiet no one could actually make out what she was saying, but a beam of light moved across the floor of the classroom and stopped at the door.

"All right, class, how about now?"

"Whoa!" Some of the kids laughed excitedly.

Izzie closed her eyes, feeling the buzz of energy below her. It surged up her body and through her chest and arms and she instantly felt renewed, more awake, and ready to continue her day as if she had just woken up from a long sleep. Her body tingled from the top of her head to the tips of her toes. Miss Grant raised the wand and whispered again, and this time the glow moved the opposite direction and the feeling of the increased energy ceased.

"Pretty cool, huh?" Miss Grant put her wand away and motioned for everyone to have a seat. "Now I must go over the rules."

"Of course, always rules," Ethan grumped.

Miss Grant smirked. "No freshmen are allowed in the underground city without being escorted by an instructor and with the express permission of the headmistress. No students are allowed in the dark parts of town. They are extremely dangerous, and you have no business there. Okay, let's open your books to page 145."

Alison flipped through her pages as some of the students behind her whispered to each other.

"I heard that the dark city was where that dark witch Rhazdon hid for years."

"I heard that if you go to the dark city and you don't have business, they will torture you and then send you topside with one or more limbs missing."

"My uncle works for the Silver Griffins in Chicago and he says that there are areas in the dark city where you can be thrown into the World in Between."

Izzie turned around and looked at the three boys. "What's that?"

"It's the place between life and death. You can be there for centuries and only watch your loved ones from inside, never talking to them. There are dark creatures that hunt you. Our headmistress was there for like fourteen years, but her granddaughter broke her out, which until that point was unheard of."

"Sounds like a story to scare kids." Izzie chuckled and rolled her eyes.

Miss Grant slapped her hand on Izzie's book, staring down at her with a serious face.

"I can assure you, Izzie, that the World in Between is anything but a scary story. It is a real place, and we have lost many to its dark magic. Don't forget that."

15

Izzie walked down the corridor that led from the library to the dorms. She had spent the afternoon studying her textbooks, her mind weaving in and out of focus. There was a spark of excitement in the air, at least for the other students. Parents' Weekend was in only two days and the place would be flooded again with magical proud moms and dads, coming to see what their kids had been learning. It was great for everyone else but left a knot in Izzie's stomach.

Izzie sighed and turned the corner into the common area of the lowerclass girls' dorms. The room was loud and busy and there were girls all over the place. Some were studying, some hanging out talking and laughing, and others showed off their Parents' Weekend attire. Everyone wanted to look their best, and it was an excuse to get out of their drab uniforms for a change. Izzie tried to ignore it and went to her room, but it was the same in there. Kathleen stood next to her mirror with a long yellow sundress perfectly draped over her figure. She smiled at herself, fluffing her hair and letting it fall gracefully over her shoulders.

"Izzie, you're back. We were just discussing what we would be wearing this weekend. What do you have stashed back there in the closet?"

"Actually..." Izzie set her bag down on the bed and turned sheepishly toward Kathleen. "I was kind of hoping one of you had something that I could borrow."

Kathleen eyed her. "Everything I have would be too long on you. I'm a bit taller."

"I have something," Emma called, rushing to her closet. "And I think it would fit your personality perfectly."

Emma searched through her closet and pulled out a long blue sundress with a silver edging along the bottom. Izzie smiled and took the dress quickly changing into it. She looked at the girls, who all smiled excitedly. The dress fit her perfectly, billowing at the top and cinching at the waist with elastic. The bottom touched the ground and the silver shimmered. Emma grabbed a pair of silver sandals, handing them to Izzie.

"These will go perfectly."

"Thank you."

Izzie smiled and glanced at Alison, who was sitting on the edge of her bed. She looked sad, staring at the floor not participating at all with the other girls. Izzie remembered Alison telling her that her mother was dead. Izzie turned back to Emma.

"This really is kind of you. I wouldn't have anything to wear otherwise."

"No problem. It's a bit big for me anyway, I'm built like my mother—tiny. My grandmother got that for me, and though I love it it's still too big for me. You make it look like it's supposed to."

Izzie smiled and Emma went back to her closet, trying to piece together her outfit for the weekend. She took the dress off and carefully hung it on the back of her closet door, setting the sandals inside on the shelf. She pulled her jeans and a t-shirt on and walked over to Alison's bed, plopping down next to her.

"What do you say we take a walk? It's beautiful outside."

"Sure." Alison half-smiled.

Izzie looked at the other girls, but they were too busy to notice. Izzie and Alison headed out through the droves of girls all laughing and talking excitedly. They went out the front doors of the mansion and headed through the pasture, waving at the caretaker as they took the path to the woods. Alison didn't say anything at first, just focused on putting distance between herself and all the talk and excitement of the upcoming weekend.

The sun shone brightly on them, the rays of light seeping down through the canopy of the forest. The air had cooled a bit, but it was still warm enough to walk around without a jacket. Fall would hit them soon, and then the more trying holidays like Thanksgiving and Christmas. Alison didn't even want to think about it; she just wanted to relax. When they reached the stream, they picked a nice piece of moss and took a seat.

Izzie leaned back on her hands, tilting her head up toward the light. Her energy moved and changed. Alison could tell there was something on her mind since her energy was slightly off, but she wanted to give her the chance to bring it up first, if at all. She knew first-hand how hard it was to talk about things like that. The girls sat quietly, watching the different types of birds fly around and listening to the trickling of the stream. After a half hour Izzie sat up, pulled her knees to her chest, and rested her chin on them.

"I don't remember a lot about being a kid." She stared into the distance and Alison sat up, twisting a twig in her fingers and just listening. "My memories of the orphanage are almost like a movie playing in my head; there's no real emotion behind them. There was a school there, and humans, but I was the only one with a magical background. They didn't tell me, though, so I can remember strange things happening and me thinking I was going crazy."

"Did they tell you anything about your parents?"

"Not that I can remember. Sometimes it feels like I never had any; like I was just made out of thin air. There isn't a single memory of them."

As Izzie sat there thinking about her past, Alison could see strange orange and black streaks twisting through her energy. Anytime a new memory—which Alison saw as yellow—popped into her energy the orange and black would swirl around it, almost as if it were choking it. She had never seen something like that before and wasn't quite sure what was going on.

"I just keep thinking that maybe they are out there somewhere looking for me. Or maybe they had to give me up and they are on Oriceran waiting for the portal to open."

Alison smiled gently. "Maybe. For me there is already closure: my mother is dead."

"I'm sorry." Izzie looked at her with embarrassment. "I never meant to make you feel bad."

"You didn't. I've gotten used to it, to a certain extent. And I have Brownstone and Shay, who are wonderful. I just don't want everyone knowing, you know? It's too dark of a past to explain to people and think that they would take it with grace. I don't need a thousand and one questions."

"I feel you there. Only you and the staff know where I came from. I won some sort of scholarship and now I am the ward of the headmistress."

"She seems nice, though."

"Ms. Berens? Oh, yeah, she's cool. Doesn't take any crap from anyone, but she is really nice."

Alison gave her a crooked smile. "But she's not your mother."

Izzie nodded, touching the top of a mushroom. "Exactly, and I have so many questions but no one to answer them. It's incredibly frustrating."

"I completely understand," Alison replied, nodding. "You want to know everything about yourself, like where you came from, but there is only so much information."

"Yep."

The girls both got quiet and stared at the stream, their minds wandering through thoughts of their parents. Alison shook her head, knowing it wasn't the time or place to relive those memories. Her mother was gone—who cared about her father!—and now she had to make her own way in the world. But then she remembered James and Shay again and cheered back up. How could she have forgotten them for a second? She was *not* alone.

"Alison? Thanks for being my friend."

"We are kind of two peas in a pod. How about we head back and go to the dining hall? I've heard you can drop in all afternoon and get ice cream sundaes."

"I love ice cream, like *obsessively* love ice cream." Izzie laughed, her energy almost back to normal.

The two girls stood up and turned to head back toward the school. Izzie looked into the dark of the forest, shaking her head.

"What's up?" Alison frowned.

"I don't know what it is, but I constantly feel like I have forgotten something. It just won't come out."

"I hate when that happens," Alison commiserated.

Izzie's energy spiked again, then calmed as she looked at Alison and shrugged.

"I guess if it's that important my mind will release it eventually."

"Yep, and even if it doesn't, your history doesn't define your life. It's the future that you make."

"That sounds like a greeting card." Izzie laughed.

"I know, right?" Alison chuckled and took Izzie's hand and pulled her back through the woods.

When they reached the mansion, they skirted quickly past Scarlett and a group of upperclassmen who had gathered and were casting magic in a circle. That was the last thing either of them needed—a run in with a group of asshole older kids. They moved through the crowded hall to the dining area, walking in to find it almost completely empty. It looked as if not many knew about the ice cream yet.

They sat down at their normal table and two bowls of plain vanilla ice cream appeared in front of them. One by one more containers appeared as well, bearing everything the girls could think of to garnish a sundae. Izzie smiled and grabbed a dish of chocolate-covered something or other.

"What is that?" Alison tilted her head in question.

"Chocolate-covered espresso beans." Izzie smiled. "I'm not sure where I had them before, but I know they are awesome in ice cream."

"Interesting, but I think I'll stick to caramel, fudge, and sprinkles."

The girls built themselves giant sundaes, smiling as a bowl of whipped cream appeared in the center. They both put a huge dollop on top of their creations, then sat back to enjoy the cool, quiet dining area. They felt almost as if they had discovered a secret.

"Enjoying your sundaes?" The headmistress winked and grabbed a handful of the chocolate-covered espresso beans. "Mmmm, I love these. Good choices, ladies. And do me a favor? Keep the ice cream social a secret."

She winked again and walked back out of the cafeteria, leaving Izzie and Alison staring at each other.

"Did she do this for us?"

Izzie shrugged and took another bite, concerned only with how delicious her ice cream was. "Maybe, but that's even better for us. I told you she was cool."

"I would have to agree." Alison laughed, taking another bite of hers.

Still, deep in her chest, she could feel the sadness. She still missed her mom.

16

The school was almost bursting at the seams. There were parents and kids all over the place. The freshmen talked loudly through the halls, showing their parents all around the mansion and introducing them to their different teachers. The headmistress had lifted the ban on magic outside the classrooms to give the kids a chance to show their parents what they had learned so far that year. The ban was pretty much useless anyway since everyone used magic on the school grounds, but she hoped it would settle some of the kids down a bit. She didn't need to take up her time reversing spells gone wrong or fixing accidents as in years past.

Ms. Berens walked quickly down the hallway, smiling at passing parents, and stopping every now and then for an introduction. She was trying to get over to the girls' dorms to visit Izzie, who would be feeling very lonely right about now. She knew Alison had invited her to hang out with her and Mr. Brownstone and Shay Carson, but Izzie had declined. It would have just rubbed in the fact that even though her mother was dead, Alison still had people who cared about her and Izzie didn't.

Izzie was lying on her bed in the blue dress reading a book when the headmistress knocked, then hurried into the room and shut the door.

Ms. Berens said kindly, "Izzie, come on—you can follow me around for a bit, and help the discombobulated parents. There is always someone who gets lost in the East Wing."

"It might have something to do with the maze." Izzie giggled.

"Precisely why they don't need to go there."

Izzie put on her silver sandals and they left the room. She walked behind the headmistress, smiling shyly at the parents passing by. She really didn't have any tasks to do or anything to keep her busy except walk—or sometimes run —to catch up with Ms. Berens. But she was definitely learning how to smile even when she didn't want to, and how to deal with the craziness of running a magic school.

Ms. Berens started moving again and Izzie raced to catch up, stopping again as a group of older kids and their parents approached.

"Ah, my upperclassman! Where are you headed?"

"We are going to go down to the city and get some stuff for classes," one of the kids said.

"And some delicious food." His mother winked.

"Mmmm, they have a delicious pasta dish down there at the Earth-side Italian Bistro. You should check it out. Have fun and be careful."

Izzie looked around the room, spotting Aya with her parents in the corner. They looked just as shy as her. Her mother's hair was pulled into a low ponytail and she was blushing, and her father was pushing up a pair of thick-rimmed brown glasses.

"I'm gonna sneak away," she whispered to Ms. Berens. "Maybe go for a walk through the pastures, get away from the craziness."

"Are you okay?"

"Yeah, fine." She put on her best fake smile. "Just want some quiet."

"Okay, come find me when you get back. The dining hall will be empty tonight because everyone goes out for food, so we can eat together and have whatever we like."

"Sounds good. I'll be back soon."

Izzie scooted quickly away and hurried down the front steps and onto the lawn, dodging the groups gathered there. She looked to the left and found Kathleen standing with her parents, everyone's bright red hair blowing in the breeze. She smiled and waved and Kathleen looked up and smiled at her, gesturing for her to come over. Izzie shook her head and faked a smile back, and took off toward the outskirts of the main grounds.

Once she reached the hill she let out a deep breath, looking down at her sandals. Her feet hurt, and she hated dressing up. Once she was out of sight she looked around, thinking of going to the stables, but she could see a large group at the edge of the barn. She sighed and squinted into the sun at the next hill over. There was Horace, working with one of the horses, his hair shining brightly. Horace was always a calming presence. Izzie knew he would be the perfect person to hang out with, since he wouldn't give her sad glances. It was obvious to everyone else that she had no one coming, and she was tired of dodging people. She didn't want to have to explain.

Horace wiped the sweat from his forehead, thankful for the fall breeze that swept over the hills. One of the newer horses was giving him a bit of a problem, nipping and biting the students, and working with it that day was the best thing he could do. He didn't want to interfere with the droves of magical folk who swarmed the building, and the headmistress knew how to get him if she needed him. A shadow blew over him and he looked up, nodding at the gargoyle soaring across the sky. As he turned back to his work he spotted Izzie standing all alone on the other hill in a blue and silver dress that was flapping in the breeze. He waved her over and she smiled, picking up the edge of her skirt to not trip, revealing her silver sandals.

Izzie jogged over, glad that Horace didn't mind her being there. He was all alone on top of the hill with the horse and a couple of dogs, who were running through the grass nipping at crickets. Horace looked strange, wearing an ill-fitted suit with horse hair stuck to the front of his pants, and his shoes shined perfectly. He also looked incredibly uncomfortable, pulling on his vest, the flower in the small breast pocket wilted. Izzie held back a chuckle, since she felt just as out of sorts as he obviously did.

"Nice tie." Izzie smiled, raising her eyebrows.

"Yeah, thanks." Horace grimaced, pulling on the tie to loosen it. "The headmistress requests I dress nicely when the parents come around. Makes it hard to work."

"Probably would help if your jacket wasn't too small on your shoulders."

"Had to borrow one from the instructors and he's a bit smaller than me."

Izzie walked up to the horse, petting it down the front of its nose. The horse settled, letting out a breath. Horace nodded, seeing that she too had a way with animals. She looked sad though, and almost as if she were running away from something.

Horace didn't want to ask her what was wrong so instead he started a story. "Years ago, there was this kid—a student here. He had a lot of talent, a lot of magical power, but he wasn't the same as everyone else. His breed, I guess you could call it—it was a dying one and it made him different from everyone else here."

Izzie looked at the woods in the distance, anger still bubbling inside of her. She hated that she couldn't be like the others, that she was all alone. She turned her head back, knowing Horace was trying to help by telling a story.

"This kid was shy around new people, but outgoing and great around people that he got comfortable with. The only problem was when he would get comfortable many of them would turn on him, teasing him about who he was and where he came from. He was in a sea of different magical creatures, but he still felt all alone."

"I can understand how that feels," she mumbled.

Horace looked across the fields at the school, where the

parents and kids were starting to clear out. He frowned and looked down at his watch, letting out a deep breath. It was nearing dinner time, and he was supposed to go back and clean up while everyone was away.

"It's five already," he grumped.

"Is it? I told Ms. Berens I would meet her for dinner. Can we continue this story another time?"

"Of course."

"Thanks, Horace, and thanks for talking."

Horace nodded and Izzie walked slowly back down the hill and toward the mansion. He grabbed the reins of the horse and walked it back over to the barn, put the animals and his tools away, and headed over to the school. He knew how it felt to be different too, but in the opposite way that Izzie did. It could get pretty lonely around here, and he hoped she wouldn't have to go through it too.

Izzie hurried through the mansion and to the dining hall to find Ms. Berens. She smiled when she found her and walked over the table.

"I thought you were gonna stand me up."

Izzie smiled. "I wouldn't do that. It's kind of you to invite me. So, what's for dinner?"

"Anything you want. Just think it, and it appears."

Izzie looked down at the empty plate in front of her and closed her eyes, musing. When she opened them, there was a giant plate of fettuccine alfredo in front of her with small tomatoes cut up on top. She grinned and picked up her fork, taking a bite.

Izzie and the headmistress spent the rest of the evening together. They ate and watched a movie, and Izzie went to bed before the other girls had gotten back. They knew if the lights were off they would be quiet when they entered, and Izzie wouldn't have to hear all about their amazing days.

As Izzie laid there waiting to fall asleep, she hoped the next day wouldn't be so stressful.

The next day was a lot like the first, only everyone was a bit calmer. The parents went to different meetings with the instructors and the kids wandered around waiting for them to return. Izzie spent the day helping the headmistress, and Alison wandered the mansion on her own since Brownstone and Shay had left. She settled into the library to do some reading. Leo Decker approached with a scowl, ready to say something, but once he saw it was Alison he left her alone with a warning.

"Just don't take any books from here." His bowler hat was tilted to the side, the flower steadily blowing raspberries and gritting its teeth. "I'll know if you do."

"Promise." Alison made a cross over her heart.

Leo harrumphed and walked back to the vault where he was working. He probably hated weekends like those as much as she did. He didn't really seem like a people person. Alison scanned the shelves of books, feeling the spines for the raised dots, pulling down different spell books and one on the history of magical beings. She figured if she was a Drow and not many people understood them, she should probably continue to research on her own. She took the books back to the table and opened the magical beings book, flipping through the pages until she found a picture of a man with silver hair just like her mother's. The word "Drow" was written in fancy cursive at the top of the page.

Alison read aloud to herself since there was no one else in the library to disturb.

"'The name 'Drow' is a subtext of troll, which are distant relatives. The ancient Drow were seen as dark elves, some very talented in dark magic. They worked and lived in a system of underground caves and castles, and were especially well versed in working with metals. As the Drow became more skilled, they became feared by many in the light and ultimately dwindled in number. Current day Drow are hard to find, living and moving in the shadows.' Interesting."

Alison turned the page, finding a picture of a queen Drow, her features similar to her mother's.

"'Drow tend to have darkened skin, though it starts out light like a Light Elf's. Pigmentation increases with age. Their hair becomes fully white when they reach maturity, and some royal Drow have been known to have bright silvery wisps throughout their childhoods.'"

Alison moved on from that section and flipped through, trying to find information on their magical abilities. She didn't know what she was fully capable of. She had moved things around a room, but she knew that was just the tip of the iceberg. She flipped to another page and stopped, finding a short section on powers.

"'The Drow's powers were never fully known. They were capable of many things, including casting spells to confuse opponents.' Confuse opponents? What does that mean?"

That was all there was regarding the Drow. She closed the book and sighed, since whoever had written it didn't know that much about the Drow either. She learned more than she knew before, but it only opened more questions for her.

"Whatcha reading?"

Alison jumped, grabbing her book and shoving it under a stack of magical spell books. Emma was behind her.

"Oh, nothing, just passing the time. Where are your parents?"

"They are finishing up a meeting with Ms. Berens. I saw you in here, so I figured I would come see how you are doing."

"I'm okay. Just getting through the rest of the weekend. I'm sad they left early, but it was great to see them. But now I'm ready to hit the books again."

Emma nodded, obviously wanting to ask but not wanting to upset her. Leo groaned in the background as he carried another book back to the vault. He grumbled something to himself as he walked.

"Do you want to come see the new plants with me? Someone said they can sing."

Alison smiled. "Sure. Let me just put these away so the librarian doesn't have me for lunch."

Emma giggled and helped Alison collect her books, ignoring the magical creatures book at the bottom. They hurried over and put each one back exactly where it was supposed to go, then looked up at the big clock over the doors. The day had raced by, and Alison was shocked by how long she had been there. It had felt like only an hour, but it was almost evening.

"They put a spell on the library," Emma explained. "It helps to keep you focused, but you can definitely lose time here. I heard about an upperclassman who missed his finals since he lost all track of time. They finally found him half-starved in the corner, reading through a potions book on the last day of school."

"Ugh…death by education."

The girls headed down the hallway to the main area as a crowd of students and parents walked toward the plants area. Emma wrinkled her nose and looked at Alison.

"It's busy."

"Yeah." Alison scoffed. "Maybe I'll catch them another time."

"Oh, look, two little freshmen without their mommies and daddies," Scarlett called from the side with a laugh, putting her fingers to her lips. "Now, let me see. I saw you and your chubby little parents. It makes so much sense why you eat carrots at every meal."

"Shut up," Emma growled.

"Just ignore her. She's insecure," Alison whispered.

Scarlett's face dropped for a moment, wondering how she could possibly know something like that. She regained her composure just as fast and clenched her fists. She stared at the silver tips of Alison's hair, her frown turning into a smirk.

"That's rich coming from the lonely one with no mommy and daddy."

Alison narrowed her eyes and gritted her teeth, trying to ignore her.

"Rumor has it you don't even have a family. Maybe you are the one who should be ignored. Pathetic girl. No one will want a nasty dark troll working for them. This is all a waste of your time."

The group laughed and Alison turned toward Scarlett, her eyes almost glowing with anger. As she stepped forward there was a surge of energy inside of her.

Emma's eyes dropped to Alison's rolled-up pant legs, where purple flames began to spark and shimmer, slowly rising upward. She was the only one who had noticed, and they didn't seem to hurt Alison at all.

"What is this?" The headmistress barreled toward the girls, putting one hand on Alison's shoulder.

Immediately Alison snapped out of it and the flames disappeared. Ms. Berens looked at Alison and then at Scarlett, obviously irritated, but concerned after seeing the flames rushing up Alison's legs.

"Scarlett, why does it not surprise me that you would be involved in this? Go…shoo! Your mother and father will be moved up in my conference schedule. I don't want any more trouble out of you."

Scarlett rolled her eyes and glanced one last time at Alison before marching off with the others. Ms. Berens turned to Alison and put her hands on her shoulders.

"Are you all right?"

"I'm fine." Alison stepped back with tears burning in her eyes. "I just want to be alone."

Alison headed for the front door and Emma reached out to her.

"Alison, wait!"

Alison shut the front door behind her with a slam.

Miss Berens looked at Emma with a kind smile. "She will be all right, just give her some space. She will come around, I promise."

"Edgar," Horace yelled at the brown hound that was running ahead of him.

The other dogs searched the ground below, following different scents. Horace held a bright lantern in his hand and was roving the grounds, making sure no one was where they weren't supposed to be. He did it every night, sometimes finding kids, but usually just finding some weird creature or plant that had escaped from one of the classrooms. It wasn't like Edgar to run off so Horace picked up the pace, heading for the small garden building ahead. He rounded the corner and stopped when he found Edgar busy licking Izzie's face and she was chuckling.

"Edgar, let the girl breathe." Horace reached down and helped Izzie to her feet.

"Thanks."

"What are you doing out here in the dark? It's not always safe."

"I know." Izzie sighed and her smile faded. "I just needed some air and some time to walk around. I couldn't sleep, and I didn't want to interrupt the girls."

"Well, I do this roving watch. You're welcome to walk along with me. I'd prefer that over you wandering around on your own."

Izzie nodded her thanks and started walking next to Horace, Edgar pacing close to her legs. She had been warned about the possible dangers of being out at night, but for some reason, she felt more comfort in the dark than the light. On top of that, she didn't sleep well anymore. She ended up tossing and turning and staring at the ceiling until she finally just gave up and wandered around.

"So what happened to that student you were telling me about?"

"Oh, well a lot actually." Horace helped Izzie down over a fallen tree stump. "This student hated being teased for being different, but instead of toning it down, they went to great lengths to prove their individuality. I think this student thought if people thought the student was special instead of different things would go differently for them. The student studied and studied, trying different spells, different potions, and anything else they could do. The student actually got pretty talented at potion making, but the results were never light; they were always a bit on the revenge side."

"Like what?"

"Spells to make people do poorly on tests, ones that incapacitated other students so they didn't enjoy an event or field trip, and other malicious stuff."

"Did the students deserve it?"

"They were the bullies, but at the same time it wasn't that student's place to dole out punishments and every time that others completed a spell, watched it unfold, and received praise and worship for the work they did, the student grew darker and darker."

Horace walked Izzie to the edge of the front steps, looking up at the window he remembered the student standing in late at night. He turned back to Izzie and took Edgar's leash from her.

"Eventually, rumors started to spread that this student had turned to dark magic, the kind that we don't even allow anywhere near our school. It's true that there needs to be a balance between dark and light in order for magic to survive, but they said that this person had dived in head first."

"I don't understand why?" Izzie replied. "I mean, just walk away, or transfer to another school. Anything, really."

"Not everyone can see that." Horace looked up as the front doors opened, The headmistress stood there with a lamp in her hand, dressed in a robe. Horace nodded at her.

"She couldn't sleep and started wandering around, so she tagged along with me and the dogs."

Izzie looked at the headmistress.

"Sorry, I just wanted some air and to be away from the others."

"Well, I hope you got what you needed, and now you can go back to bed, dear. Come on."

Izzie smiled at Horace, thankful that she had run into him. "Finish the story another time?"

"Of course. Good night."

Mara stepped to the side as Izzie walked inside and went up the stairs. She turned back to Horace with a concerned look on her face.

"She will be okay," Horace told her. "Just give it some time."

Mara nodded, thinking about her granddaughter Leira and how strange everyone had thought she was. It hadn't been until she had understood her heritage and her powers that she had learned to accept herself. She could only hope the same went for Izzie.

A couple of weeks had gone by since the Parents' Weekend and everything was back to normal. Fall was setting in and the leaves on the trees over the stream were turning bright shades of orange and red. The girls were lying around on the patches of moss talking about the latest happenings. Ethan was perched on a large boulder to the side, whittling a stick with his unauthorized knife. Peter swung back and forth on the tire, grabbing the ropes and leaning back and looking up at the blue sky through the treetops.

"Claire can't stop talking about the kemana and her trips to the city." Kathleen rolled her eyes; she was jealous. "It's so annoying that idiots like her and Scarlett are allowed down there but we aren't."

"One of the older boys was showing off a new jewelry box he bought for his girlfriend. Every time you open it a new piece of jewelry appears," Peter shouted as he swung higher. "Then Berens took it away. Apparently the jewelry was being stolen from different magical beings and placed there. He was a bit upset."

"Serves him right." Aya shook her head. "Shouldn't be buying stuff from the merchants there. Everyone knows they get their stuff from the Willen. Those little creatures steal anything that's not nailed down."

Emma laughed. "I think they're cute."

"Until they steal *your* stuff."

Kathleen leaned back, her hands on the moss behind her. "I just want to go and see all the clothes. I heard there are cloaks there made of unicorn hair."

Peter jumped down from the swing with a thud and wiped the dust off his hands. "And the food. I heard you can get any kind of food you would ever want."

"What is it with boys and food?" Kathleen wrinkled her nose.

Across the moss, Alison was almost in a trance. As she stared up at the swaying canopy, she felt almost disconnected from her body. The voices of her friends were just background noise, like she was floating in some sort of dream world. Everything was calm and comforting, and she felt her body recharging.

"Maybe it's just me, but I think it's time to bend a few rules." Ethan jumped down from the boulder and closed his knife against his leg, sticking it in his pocket. "We should go to the city. I mean, what can really happen that hasn't happened to me living on the streets for so long?"

Aya's eyes grew big. "Expulsion, arrest... Death!"

"Eh." Ethan waved his hands and stuck them in his pockets. "They won't find out; not unless we are stupid about it. We can't just go grandstanding in there, and we can't come back flashing a bunch of new stuff."

Kathleen lifted an eyebrow. "I don't know. It sounds really risky. What do you think, Alison? Alison?"

Kathleen leaned over and touched Alison's leg, breaking her trance. She gasped and sat up, then stretched her arms out, feeling very well rested—almost as if she had slept for an entire night. It was a strange feeling, and she wondered how she had managed to do it. She slowly focused on the others, who were staring at her in amusement.

"I'm sorry, what did you ask me?"

"The underground city. Should we go? Ethan thinks we should throw caution to the winds and head down there."

"I mean, it's against the rules buuuut...I'm in." Alison shrugged, figuring there were worse rules they could break.

"I'm in too." Izzie stood up. "I mean, I'm sick and tired of hearing all the stories from the upperclassman and having them dangle their new trinkets and stuff in our faces."

"That's what *I'm* talkin' about." Ethan rubbed his hands together and bit his bottom lip. "I think we stand by and wait, watching the ones who are going for the day. We follow them to the entrance, and once they've gone in we go in behind them. No one will even notice we're gone. We can go in, do whatever we want, then sneak back out and be back for dinner. No problem."

Everyone was on board and they stared at Aya, who Alison could tell by her energy was having trouble with the idea of breaking the rules. Finally she let her hands fall to her sides.

"Fine, I'm in. I can't be the only one who hasn't been down there."

Peter jumped up and down excitedly. Ethan laughed and shook his head at Aya. He liked the idea of her loosening up a bit.

"Okay, so we should go back to our rooms and get ready." Ethan grabbed his bag. "Everyone meets behind the mansion. The kemana is in the caves behind the school and stretches out for miles in every direction. That's where we'll find the stairway."

The girls all stood up and nodded at Ethan, watching him and Peter run off into the woods. Aya looked at them and crossed her arms. Kathleen laughed and walked over, putting her arm around Aya's shoulder.

"Relax, girl, this is going to be an adventure. Besides, you don't want to go your whole high school career and never do anything fun or exciting. I promise you that if you do you will totally regret it."

Aya sighed and nodded. "You're right. I need to live a little. Besides, my mom described a necklace down there and said she was hoping to get it next time she was in town. I'd like to send it to her."

"Perfect! All right, ladies, let's go get ready. Adventure awaits!"

Peter, Ethan, Emma, Izzie, Kathleen, Alison, and Luke stood at the opening of the caves, all a bit nervous. In the end, Aya had changed her mind, not wanting to get in trouble and *really* not wanting to break the rules. Kathleen had given up trying to convince her and pulled the other girls along before they too could change their minds.

"I'll cover for you if anyone notices you're gone," Aya had told the group.

Kathleen pulled her hair back into a ponytail and took a deep breath, looking down the line at Ethan but stopping at Luke.

"What's the dog doing here?"

Luke rolled his eyes and Ethan patted him on the back. "He's a good guy and he's coming along for the ride. Chill."

"Whatever."

The group moved into the caves, hiding behind several large stones and peering between them as the older students opened the door to the kemana and disappeared behind it. Once they were out of sight, everyone stood up and walked over to the round stone circle on the wall. There were several symbols all with glowing white light behind them. Emma shook her head.

"If we don't know the code we can't get in."

Kathleen scoffed. "We'll guess."

"No! Really bad things happen when you don't use the right code to get into the kemana. Surges of electricity, falling rocks, and I've heard even tears in the World In Between."

Ethan stepped forward with a smile, waving a piece of paper in his hand. "Luckily I managed to swipe this from Mr. Regency while he was taking a whiskey-fueled nap earlier. It's the kemana code."

Kathleen nodded with an impressed look on her face. "You are worth your annoyance sometimes."

"I'll take that as a compliment."

Ethan unfolded the paper and started to press the stones in order, careful not to make any mistakes. He wanted to go to the underground city, but not badly enough to get one of his friends smashed by a boulder. When he was done, he took a step back and everyone looked around, waiting.

"Maybe you didn't press them hard enough?" Izzie wrinkled her nose.

"No, just give it a second."

Not even a second later the ground began to shake, and small pieces of rock and dust drifted down. A large stone door appeared and the sound of scraping stone echoed as the door slid open to reveal a long dark staircase. The wall to the right glowed where the vibrant crystal of the kemana was embedded. Small crystals on the ceiling led off into the darkness, and as Ethan stepped forward the crystal lit up, creating light down the stairs and around a corner.

"Wow, look at that energy. It's beautiful." Alison was amazed at the colors.

With Alison in the back, they edged down the stone staircase one step at a time. Alison ran her hand over the wall, seeing the bright magical light of the kemana. It was the ultimate Energizer battery, only instead of mechanical bunnies the thing powered the magical community, including the school. It was beautiful and powerful.

As they moved farther down the winding staircase, they began to hear the echoes of people talking. Izzie looked back nervously at Alison, but she just gave her a reassuring smile. Alison was no stick-in-the-mud, but she had never really been a rule-breaker. This was exciting; something that reminded her of her old life, which felt like it had been a lifetime ago. She was surrounded by magic, and there was something about the dark tunnel that made her feel like she was home.

When they reached the bottom, they walked through a large archway with the name "Ruby Falls" etched into the stone and looked out in awe at the bustling little city. There were magical creatures everywhere, all of them in their true magical form. Shops lined the streets and the various fragrances of delicious food wafted through the air. The ceiling was like the one in the mansion, magically created to show night and day.

"At night the sky looks like Oriceran's, complete with the two moons," Emma whispered.

Izzie was in awe, watching the creatures sweep the floors, barter, and even drink at a small pub to the side. She had never seen anything like that—at least not that she could remember. It didn't surprise her, though. She had grown up in a non-magical orphanage, so obviously they hadn't taken any field trips to magical underground cities.

"Do these people live here?"

Ethan looked at her. "Many of them do. I heard they got tired of trying to conform to what the humans felt comfortable with, so they moved down here. They don't have to enchant their skin, they maintain a constant charge of their magic, they are among their people, and they can make the place feel like home. Apparently not all of them found Earth to be all that it was cracked up to be when they came through the portal."

"I can understand wanting to be with your own people," Alison mumbled, ignoring Kathleen's side glance.

There were a lot of magical creatures there, but she still

didn't see anyone with Drow energy. She pulled her hair back and twisted the ends under into a messy bun. If the book was right and people were afraid of her kind, she wanted to make sure no one had a clue that she was a Drow. She didn't need the entirety of the underground city chasing her with pitchforks and torches—not when it was her first time there. She now understood what these upperclassmen were so excited about.

"All right, guys let's go see everything. Don't lose each other, just in case." Ethan stepped forward but stopped. "Oh, and if you see any instructors or upperclassman, send a ball of light into the sky. Don't worry, I got you, Luke. And damn, *have some fun.*"

19

The group walked into the town, smiling at the vendors as they attempted to wave them over. They had carts and carts full of trinkets, stones, and old books. On the corner was a café with a large cup of coffee on the sign and the effect of steam rising through magic into the artificially cloudy sky. Ethan stopped in front of an old trading post, a shop with lots of different items all mixed up in the window. A massive rough-skinned Kilomea walked past them grumbling something in another language. Emma jumped and grabbed Peter's arm and then released it, her cheeks red with embarrassment.

"This is where you trade your money in," Ethan explained. "You can't use Earth dollars here."

He pointed to a sign that read, "Trade Dollars for Ruby Coins." It was the currency of Ruby Falls. The group entered the small store, forming a line behind a large Crystal. His body was made of ice crystals that hung from him. Izzie was the closest to him, and she shivered from the cold coming from his body. You could see her breath puffing from her nostrils as her lips changed color.

"Did it just get cold in here?"

"That's me," the Crystal replied, looking back at her. "Sorry about that, kids."

Izzie smiled nervously. "It's okay."

She turned back to the group with wide eyes and they all had to stifle a laugh.

Izzie looked to her right, reading a sign out loud. "'Welcome to Ruby Falls.'"

Alison lifted her chin. "I wonder why they call it that?"

"Uh, probably because the kemana has bright red crystals like a ruby? Couldn't you see that coming in?" Kathleen looked at her strangely.

"Oh, yeah." Alison chuckled and turned away, the smile fading from her lips. She had seen the energy of the stone, which was pure white light. She couldn't, however, see what the stone actually looked like. To her, the walls were just an unbroken stretch of shimmering magic. The same went for the crystals on the ceiling of the staircase—they had glowed white as well. She forgot sometimes that not everyone saw the world the way she did, but it was not the time or the place for her to start trying to explain that to the group.

Everyone but Ethan traded some of their money for the round gold coins with Ruby Falls stamped on them. Alison and Izzie shoved their coins into their pockets, while the others bought small velvet bags from the counter and tied them to their belts. They headed into the street, looking around at all the different options.

"I want to go to the woodworking shop, I hear they

have awesome whittling knives." Ethan pointed down the street.

Kathleen looked at a dress shop and smiled. "Come on, Emma, let's hit that one."

Emma grinned and followed Kathleen. Peter had already wandered into a bookstore next to the annex, which left Luke, Alison, and Izzie standing there staring at each other. Luke chuckled uncomfortably and just turned around and walked away, giving a nearby Gnome a nasty look as he left.

Alison looked at Izzie. "Well, where do you want to go?"

"I saw a cool general store when we were walking in. We can start there and work our way down."

"Sounds perfect to me."

Alison and Izzie walked back down the block and perused the shelves of the general store. They both bought small trinkets—a necklace with moving pictures inside its locket, small stones said to be carved from the kemana itself, and Alison picked up a pen that shot magic text out to save your hand from writing so much. They put their prizes in their pockets and moved on, stopping at the café to try one of their cherry tarts. The food was delicious; more amazing than anything Izzie could remember eating aboveground, even that ice cream sundae.

"I'm sure the chef uses a bit of magic to make it taste that way." Alison took a bite of hers and cherry dripped down her chin.

"Yeah, it's probably all magic. We're likely eating sawdust and paste."

Across the way Peter walked through the bookstore, astonished at all the books on magic. Almost all of them had come directly from Oriceran, unlike the ones his father had given him that had been reprinted on Earth. He ran his fingers down the spines, watching the titles shimmer and move as his energy mixed with the book's. As he passed a book of spells he stopped, feeling a jolt of energy shoot up his arm.

"That means the book has chosen you," the elderly shopkeeper told him, looking over his glasses. "They have minds of their own."

Peter nodded and pulled the book from the shelf, flipping open the pages. It had been written by hand, or at least it looked that way. There were spells and counter-spells from the old days of magic, long before Oricerans had brought it to Earth. The book intrigued Peter, so he closed it and walked up to the shopkeeper, pulling out his coin purse. As he waited for his change he noticed Ethan standing just inside the woodworking shop.

He picked up a knife and read the attached card, "Pour your energy through the knife creating artistic works not seen anywhere but Oriceran. Wow your human friends and decorate your cottage."

Ethan flipped the tag over and looked at the price. He didn't have any money, or at least not enough for the knife. The woodworker walked into the back room, closing the curtain behind him. Ethan looked out at the street and saw Peter watching. He smiled mischievously, tucked the knife in his pocket, and joined Peter in the bookstore.

"Your change." The shopkeeper handed Peter some coins and the book wrapped in paper and tied with a black string.

"Thanks." Peter and Ethan exited and stood to the side. "I saw you take that."

Ethan shrugged. "It's ingrained in me. Besides, I don't have people to just give me money. My aunt and uncle came to Parents' Weekend and didn't leave me a dime. Assholes."

"At least you *had* someone," Peter said as Izzie and Alison walked toward them.

"Yeah, I guess you're right."

Kathleen and Emma ran across the cobblestone walk with several bags of clothes on their arms. "Hey, guys."

"When are you even going to wear those clothes?" Ethan rolled his eyes.

"Whenever I don't have to wear my uniform, I don't care if it's just in the dorm room studying. I'll take any chance to get out of that hideous thing!"

"I got a book on old spells." Peter held up the paper-wrapped book. "It's really awesome."

Izzie cleared her throat, still holding a chunk of her cherry tart. "There's a spot one of the store owners told me about, right on the edge of the nice part of town." She pointed down the street. "Down and to the left. Apparently you get a really awesome view of the cavern from there."

"Cool." Ethan waved his arms. "Let's go see it."

Alison looked around. "Where's Luke?"

"I dunno, probably with his people planning our destruction." Kathleen laughed to herself. "We'll find him before we go."

The group walked through the ritzier part of town, where all the houses were separated by white picket fences. Most of them were carved into the side of the cavern and enchanted to look like they all imagined the cottages in Oriceran did, only about three times the size. When they reached the edge of town they stopped, agog at the view. There were stones and rocks jutting up from the ground as far as the eye could see with the ruby red of the kemana shining through. Of course, to Alison, it looked like bright white light coming through the cracks, but it was still beautiful.

A tingle began to move through Alison's fingers and into her chest and she rubbed the spot with her hand, figuring the cherry tart had given her indigestion. Izzie looked at her, furrowing her brow, then walked over and stood next to her.

"You okay?"

"Yeah, I just have indigestion. Must be the sawdust and glue." Alison chuckled.

"No, I mean because of the weird darkness swirling at your ankles."

Alison looked down at her feet. She had somehow created a darkness around herself. She had never done anything like that, and wasn't sure why it was happening now. Then out of nowhere she heard a cracking sound, like a falling tree. She turned quickly, threw a flash of light, and batted away a fireball that was heading straight for Izzie's head. When they looked up three young dark wizards stood there with their hoods pulled over their heads. The one in the center clapped briefly, then stepped forward with his hand around his wand.

"Haven't they told you kids not to come so close to the dark territory?"

"We don't want any trouble." Ethan stepped forward, his chest puffed out.

The wizards all laughed loudly and glanced at each other. The leader stared at the group, his eyes shining. "Too late."

He cast a beam of light out of his wand and without thinking Alison lunged in front of it, sending out tiny orbs of light that absorbed the magic. Ethan and Alison rolled across the ground as Izzie began to fight back. She threw her hands out, pulling energy from the ground. Symbols flashed across her skin and she shot bolts of lightning from her hands, catching one of the wizards' cloaks ablaze. The others did the best they could, using what they had learned in class to defend themselves.

Alison and Izzie stood side by side throwing magic at the wizards. When Alison twisted her hand around purple flames engulfed her fingers and she hurled them at the leader, sending him up in flames. He couldn't feel them, but it blinded him long enough for Izzie to launch a giant fireball. It hit him in the chest and knocked him backward into the other two. They slid across the black stone and Alison looked encouragingly at Izzie.

"I thought you didn't know a lot of magic."

"I thought so too." Izzie shrugged as the wizards picked themselves back up. The leader rushed forward and sent out a bolt of dark energy that wrapped around Alison's arm. She looked at it, then at the wizard, and shook her arm. The magic had no effect on her. The wizard narrowed his eyes and considered her for a moment, then fired another stream, then another, but she shook each one off with no damage.

"It can't be," he whispered.

Alison wanted to know what he meant; wanted to know why what she was doing was so strange and unusual that he stopped in his tracks. Izzie sent waves of magic out that slammed into the other two wizards, knocking their wands from their hands. Ethan and the others cheered as the wizards scrambled for their wands.

The leader of the group was still staring at Alison and kept testing his magic on her until she balled her hands into fists and slashed them through the air in front of her, creating a wave of darkness that rushed toward the wizard. He ducked and it flew past.

"You... You are *her*!"

Just then there was a loud howl from behind them and Izzie jumped next to Alison as a werewolf came barreling toward them, teeth bared.

20

The wolf was large and black and its eyes glowed bright yellow. It snarled and growled as it moved toward them, its sharp vicious teeth dripping saliva. Alison narrowed her eyes and stepped forward, seeing the energy of the beast as its muscles tensed and moved.

Izzie was trying to pull her back. "Wait," she whispered.

The beast was familiar, and she could feel this pull toward him like they were connected in some way. As he got closer he leapt over Izzie and pounced on the wizard leader, and they rolled across the ground. Alison spun to watch the two souls battle. The wolf looked back at Alison and she knew that wasn't just some strange shifter—it was Luke.

He turned back to the wizard and growled, then put one immense paw across the wizard's throat to hold him down and used the other to shake the wand from his grip. Izzie pushed a stream of energy in front of her, blasting it straight into the chest of an approaching wizard who had recovered his wand. His wand flew up and magic swirled from the tip and nicked Luke in the ear, and he winced and pulled back just enough for the wizard to get his knees up and push Luke off him.

Alison froze as blood trickled down into Luke's fur, matting the hair and Izzie grabbed her arm and shook her out of her trance. The wizards had gathered again, and though they looked worse for wear they weren't backing down. Luke got up on all fours and went to Alison and Izzie, looping around Alison to protect her. He seemed to be drawn to her just as much as she was to him, and it was confusing them both. At that moment, though, there was no time for questions; the wizards were preparing for another attack.

The others were gathered together behind them, casting as much magic as they could muster. Ethan shook his head, looking at the burn mark on Peter's shirt.

"This doesn't make any sense. Sure, the dark wizards are dangerous, but they don't just go around attacking in the streets."

"Times are different now. Magic is coming to Earth and the dark beings are getting bolder." Peter was out of breath, and though the kemana recharged their magical powers they were all exhausted.

Alison nodded at Izzie when she felt the energy burning through her. Izzie lowered her hands and pulled light magic around her body and into the palms of her hands. Alison looked down at Luke and circled her hand in front of her chest, releasing small balls of light and cast them between her group and the dark beings. The orbs danced, creating a show of sparkling energy around them. The dark wizard growled and threw a fireball at Alison, and one of her orbs opened like a mouth and swallowed the dark magic.

With every dark fireball he threw Alison's orbs grew larger, until there was a solid screen of light between the group and the dark wizards. On the other side the wizards just gripped their wands, unsure what would come next. The leader squinted his eyes to stare at movement in the center of the wall of light, where tiny purple flames danced in a circle. He paused, then his eyes grew wide as Luke jumped through and bit down on his arm.

When the wizard screamed in pain, Alison dissolved the orbs and Izzie released bolts of energy one after another, foiling the wizards' attempts to fight back. Luke lost his grip when the lead wizard punched him hard in the head, but when he shook the stars from his eyes the wizard's wand was at his feet. He picked the wand up in his mouth and gave the dark being a toothy smile. The boy pulled his hood back, revealing bright white hair and ice-blue eyes.

"Do it and I will hunt down every one of your shifter kin and murder them," the wizard hissed through gritted teeth.

Luke gave him a big wolfish smile and bit down hard, splintering the wizard's wand. Dark energy seeped from the pieces as Luke spat them onto the ground, then he growled and backed toward Alison. Orbs of dark and light flew around them as Izzie and Alison attempted to push back the other wizards. Everyone was tired, but Alison's energy pushed her to keep fighting. Sweat poured down

Izzie's forehead as she pushed light from her body, spiraling the bolts at the two other wizards.

"I don't know how long I can keep this up," Izzie yelled.

"I know," Alison wheezed.

Just then, as if someone were listening, there was a rustle from the left. The bushes around them shook as some Willen—three-foot rodent-like creatures who were known as artful thieves and could hide their bounty in the folds of their skin—stepped out. They walked on their hind legs, but their bodies resembled those of oversized rats, and some wore fitted waistcoats. Others wore pearls or caps on their heads, but most wore only a charming smile on their faces. The largest of the Willen stepped out first, putting his paws in the air.

"Dirty rats," the wizard spat.

"Watch your tongue, little wizard. Five bucks says your father would happily pay for information putting his son in the center of an underground dark city fight."

The wizard looked at the Willen, then at Alison, unsure what to say. The other wizards lowered their wands as Willen surrounded them, scurrying between their feet and staring at them with their warm brown eyes. Willen loved information. Their dream was to know everything.

They were an honorable kind of thief, and they never lied and would bargain away the very shoes off their feet if it got them a gold coin or two.

"Don't think I didn't see you in the dark alleys looking for trouble." The Willen narrowed his eyes. "That information… Oh yes, that would bring a pretty penny."

"I'll kill you where you stand."

Izzie held up the bright orb on her palm. "The hell you will."

The Willen patted Izzie on the leg. "It's all right, little elf. He knows we never lie."

The wizard just stood for several moments, grinding his teeth together and staring at the Willen around them. There had to be at least a hundred, their sharp little claws tapping against the black stones beneath their feet. Finally, with a growl, the leader glared at Izzie, Luke, and finally Alison.

"This isn't over, Drow."

The lead Willen's head snapped to Alison, his eyes narrowing. The leader of the group snatched one of the other wizard's wands, then swirled it and pushed the Willen back. The wizards ran for the dark alleys in the distance, leaving the rest of them staring down at the furry creatures.

"Thank you." Alison released her magic back into the ground.

The Willen sniffed around her, ignoring the growls of the werewolf, then looked up at Alison in curiosity.

"Hmmm, a Drow. Very peculiar indeed."

Izzie looked to her right as another large Willen stepped forward, staring at her familiarly. Another Willen whispered something in his ear and his expression became one of shock. She turned toward the furry being, wanting to ask him how he knew her, but as she stepped toward him the Willen scurried in all directions, the large one mixing in with the rest.

"Be careful, young magical ones," the head Willen

warned, still gazing at Alison. "The Darkness is approaching, and you are not safe here."

With that her furry savior scampered off, running back to the darker part of town where the sun never shone and the residents liked it just fine that way. Luke groaned and when she looked down he'd shifted back to his naked human form. She helped him to his feet and for a moment the two stared at each other, unsure of what happened or what even to say about it. Luke's ear was bleeding and the hair on the side of his head was matted down.

"Are you okay?"

"Yeah." He touched his ear. "Looks worse than it is. Just a nick really. No big deal."

"Good lord, what was that?" Ethan walked forward slapping Luke on the back and handing him his overshirt. "The three of you were like rogue magic warriors."

Kathleen stepped forward with her arm still around Emma, whose energy was fearful. "Thank you, guys! You too, Luke."

"No problem," the shifter growled.

Alison hugged Emma tightly and the girl slowly began to relax. "They are gone now. We are safe. If it weren't for Izzie..."

"I don't know where I learned to fight like that, but I'm glad I did. And Alison, you have all *sorts* of magical talents."

Kathleen smiled. "Drow usually do, but they develop over time—like your silver hair." She pointed at Alison's head, the silver tips having inched up farther on her long hair.

Alison pulled her hair forward and looked at the color, surprised how fast the white had increased. She dropped her hair and looked around at everyone. The only injuries were a small burn on Peter's shoulder and Luke's bloody ear. They had been really lucky, but Alison feared that if the wizards had been older and more powerful they would have never stood a chance. Then there were the Willen, creatures who never helped anyone—yet they had stepped into the middle of this battle and saved the day. Everything about it was odd, from the fight to the Willen.

Emma opened her bag and pulled a white handkerchief, handing it to Luke with a smile.

"I'm sorry I ever doubted you. Take this and clean up your ear."

"Thank you." Luke nodded at Emma and glanced at Alison, his eyes still glowing yellow.

Above them the lightning cracked as though there was a storm approaching, and from the dark side of town magical black clouds rolled over the sky. It was like a warning. Something distant and dark was angry, and Alison didn't doubt it had to do with those three wizards and whoever their families were. She didn't want to wait around and see what the storm brought. She'd had enough battles for one day—or for one lifetime, actually. She was just glad that her powers seemed to have a mind of their own, at least they had today.

"We should get back and get cleaned up before dinner. Hopefully no one has noticed that we are gone. It's one thing to sneak into the underground city, but it's another to have an all-out battle while we are here."

21

Luke grabbed his clothes and dressed and the group gathered their belongings, making sure they had everything. Peter unwrapped his book, since the paper on the outside was torn and burned. He shook his head and looked out over the caverns. Alison walked up to him and put her hand on his shoulder.

"Good work with those blocking spells."

Peter scoffed. "Yeah, right. Good work, you and Izzie, for keeping us alive."

"I don't know how we did it, but I know all I could think about was you guys behind us. I do have to say, I think I am about done with fun trips to the underground city."

"At least for a while." Peter winked at her and they joined the others.

Ethan put his arm out, stopping them in their tracks. In front of them was the long dark alley that led to the dark part of the city and a group of young magical beings was walking out, looking around carefully as they went. When the darkened sun hit their faces, Kathleen gasped. It was Claire, Scarlett, and several of the other upperclassman. Scarlett stopped her group when she saw Alison and the gang.

Slowly she walked over to them, her brightly colored hair pulled back into a tight ponytail. She stuffed something inside her bag and held it close as she approached. She inspected them curiously. Alison and her group were more than a little the worse for wear, but at the same time, Scarlett was coming from the dark side of the city.

"I have *so* many questions."

Alison tilted her head to the side. "Likewise."

"You are lowerclassmen. You aren't supposed to be here."

"And you are upperclassmen, forbidden to enter the dark area."

"It seems you were in some sort of fight. That must have been the noise we heard. And from the looks of your little pet pup, he got in on some of the action too."

Luke snarled, but Ethan kept his hand firmly on his shoulder.

"The kemana helps the shifters change more easily, I would watch what you say to him. He's really not in the mood."

Alison kept her eyes on Scarlett's energy, in which the colors were changing and shifting. She was nervous, determined, and confused, and she was hiding all of this under a bitch persona. Alison knew that whatever she had put in that bag was not something she wanted them or anyone outside of her circle to know about—and that meant she had a negotiable situation.

"It looks like we've reached an impasse." Scarlett shifted her stance, keeping her lips tight.

"It seems that way." Alison followed her movements and streaks of fear flowed from the older girl's energy.

"How about we make a deal? I won't tell on you freshies for being caught in the underground city or whatever fight you were in and you don't tell Berens where you saw us come from."

Alison looked over her shoulder at the others. She could tell they were all on board with her, and she knew she had the upper hand. Still, she wanted peaceful days in the halls. She just wanted to not deal with their harassment anymore.

"I think that can be arranged... *if* you and your little groupies also agree to leave us alone for the rest of the school year. No poking, prodding, teasing, or anything else. Act like you don't even see us."

Scarlett tightened her jaw, hating to be under someone else's control. However, this secret was too big and too important to be blabbed to the headmistress. She would just have to agree to the terms and hope that they, at some point, went back on their word.

"Fine. It will be like we never saw each other."

"And we'll never see each other again, at least not in a way that will make either of our lives more troublesome."

Alison held out her hand and Scarlett eyed her for a moment, gripping her bag tighter. Then she nodded, flipped her ponytail as she waltzed back to her group. She told them what she had agreed to, and Scarlett looked back and nodded before they headed back toward the center of the city. Alison let out a deep breath and Peter put his hands on her shoulders.

"You should be President one day."

"Yeah." Alison laughed uncomfortably. "Or I could just graduate and get the hell away from all the drama that seems to follow me around like an annoying little sister."

The group laughed, relieved at having had something positive happen. They walked back through the streets, all their energy gone, ignoring the glares from passersby who had heard about the fight. They traded their Ruby Falls money for Earth dollars and headed for the steps that led out of the kemana.

Luke walked alongside Alison in silence, glancing at her from time to time. He didn't know what it was, but he had sensed from the main part of the city when she was in trouble. It was like something had reached inside of him and pulled him along to look for her. When he had seen the wizards attacking, his first instinct had been to change and do whatever he could to protect her. The pull was there and he knew she felt it too, but he had no idea what it meant.

Alison looked at the crystals that made up the kemana walls and wondered if she would ever see them for what they really were. Everything in her world was changing, and she didn't like the presence of dark magic in it in the least.

Horace pulled his hood down over his bright red hair and

searched in and out of shops for Izzie and her friends. He had seen them entering the caves but hadn't been able to get there in time to stop them. They had no idea how dangerous it was for them to be there, and even more so for Alison. He knew she was a Drow and the dark magic called to her, even if she hadn't figured that out yet. During several times in history Drow had maintained a neutral position between light and dark, but rarely was a Drow *all* good.

As he stepped out of the café he looked up, hearing the familiar sound of Scarlett and Claire. He moved to the side and put his head down, not wanting them to see him. Who knew what kind of devious things they were up to? Horace had been watching them for years. As they walked by, he turned to head farther into the city, but stopped when he saw Luke exit the general store. The group was behind him, all looking slightly beat up. They were not paying attention to anything. When they drew close, Horace stepped out in front of them and pushed back his hood.

"Shit." Ethan dropped his head. "Busted."

Izzie looked at Horace and almost sighed in relief. "Horace!"

"I don't know what you were doing down here, or why you look like you were in the Great Oriceran War, but you need to get back to the surface."

No one wanted to argue with him. They didn't know whether the caretaker was going to rat them out or not, but they knew fighting with him would only make things worse. Izzie stood next to Horace until the others had passed, and they took up the rear of the little procession. She opened her mouth, but Horace raised his hand and shook his head. Several of the street merchants made nasty remarks as Horace walked past, but he ignored them. He was used to it after all those years. He was the only human permitted down in the kemana, but that didn't mean the magical beings there liked it.

"Do you remember that story I was telling you?"

"The one about the boy who was different?"

"Yes, that one."

"I do, though you never finished it."

"This boy, the one who wanted so badly for people to think he was amazing, different, outstanding? Well, he started to become more powerful, as the magic grew inside of him. Symbols started to appear on his arms."

Izzie pulled her sleeve down over her wrist, looking down at the ground.

Horace saw her wince but kept telling the story. "He was collecting a group of followers, and every day the number grew just a little bit larger. He was desperate to not be alone, and felt as if he was leading these people to something. He started using forbidden spells, which in turn pushed others away from him."

Izzie looked at a shopkeeper, who was brushing off his stairs and giving Horace nasty looks.

"Meddlesome human scum, coming down to our city."

Horace ignored him, but Izzie gave him a look, letting him know he'd better knock it off.

"Don't worry about him, or any of the others. They have a right to hate humans. We have never been very welcoming to things or beings we don't understand."

They turned the corner and headed for the staircase in the distance. Horace pulled his hood up and let out a deep breath, glad to be leaving the city. He never felt safe there, and he knew if he was ever caught in a bad situation he was as good as gone.

"Anyway, so this student—he found himself in a very bad situation that he could not solve on his own, so he turned to magic. He conjured a spell, mixing things he shouldn't have. When he cast it, the spell struck one of his only friends."

"Did they get very hurt?"

"Well, had he gone for help when it happened they could have fixed it, but he was determined to prove his worth. Instead of getting help he continued to try to fix his mistake himself, which only made things worse. His friend died that night in his arms, and though the school saw it as a mistake—an accident—this student was left with blood on his hands and a life on his conscience. That kind of thing will ruin a man, or woman, or magical being, and it did that to this kid."

"That's terrible." Izzie shook her head. "I understand pain, though. Growing up I saw quite a bit of it."

"The orphanage?"

"You know?"

"I know a lot of things."

Izzie sighed, wanting to tell him more, but she couldn't find the strength to voice it. The pain that she felt every single day of her life was almost too much for her to bear. She had thought she was moving forward, but there in the streets of the kemana it felt fresher than it had in a long time.

"You don't have to tell me if you aren't ready. Sometimes this kemana not only amplifies your powers but your pain as well. You will feel better once you get some rest." He stopped Izzie at the base of the stairs. "Just remember, no matter how bad it is or how much you want to prove you are strong, you can always ask for help."

Izzie nodded, seeing a flash of pain pass cross Horace's face. She wondered if maybe the kemana *did* affect humans, just not in the same way it affected magical beings.

2 2

They climbed out of the kemana and the cool fall air became more apparent the closer they got to the top. The sun lit the steps, but from its orange cast, Izzie knew that it had to be close to late afternoon or evening. She was ready for a shower and bed at that point, not even caring if she made it to dinner. It was the weekend, so it wasn't required that she be there. When she reached the top of the steps she looked curiously at everyone, because they were just standing there.

"What are you guys doing? Oh."

Standing in front of them was the headmistress, her cloak flowing behind her in the wind. She raised an eyebrow, almost surprised to see Izzie. Horace stepped out and pushed back his hood, holding back the surprise he felt. He hadn't planned on telling her about what they had done, figuring from the way they looked, they had learned their lesson. Ms. Berens looked at Horace and sighed.

"You went looking for them as well."

Horace bowed his head and shuffled to the side, glancing at Izzie. The headmistress crossed her arms and let her eyes roam over them. Emma stood clutching her hands together and looking down at the ground, with a streak of black soot across her cheek. Kathleen grasped her bags, standing proud and tall to the side. Ethan had his hands in his pockets and was playing with whatever was inside, waiting for the punishment to just be over with. Ms. Berens raised her eyebrows at Peter and Luke—Peter with a burn in his shirt and Luke with a bleeding head. She opened her mouth but quickly shut it, realizing it was not the right place to ask questions. She eyed Izzie and Alison with disappointment.

"Go up to the mansion and into my office at once."

The group didn't say a word, just started up the hill with their heads hung low. They passed several whispering groups of students as they headed to Ms. Berens' office, and waited outside once they got there. She opened the door with a swish of her wand and they filed in, not looking her in the eyes. All except Izzie, who stared at her like she had a question. The last thing the headmistress needed was for Izzie to start asking questions about her past.

When everyone was inside Ms. Berens shut the door, then went behind her desk and stood there tapping her wand on her palm. This was not the first time freshmen had snuck off to the city, but it was the first time they had come back looking as if they had been to war. She took a deep breath and relaxed her shoulders.

"When I lived in Texas, before I went to the World In Between, I took care of my granddaughter Leira. She is grown now, but at the time she was just a child. I learned from that, and from my own daughter, that when you tell a kid not to do something, somewhere along the way they will do it just to see why they weren't allowed to. In this case, we don't block freshman from going there because we are mean. We forbid it because you do not have the magical capability to take care of yourself if you are threatened. We learned our lesson at this school many years ago, and sadly it cost a life."

Alison and the others just stood there, not knowing what to say or do. They couldn't tell the truth about the fight, and they couldn't rat out the others either. Izzie was the only one standing with her head up, almost in defiance. She believed Ms. Berens knew more about her than she was telling, but she also knew breaking the rules and sneaking off to the kemana wasn't the way to gain Ms. Berens' trust so she could get the whole story.

"I am assuming you went there because you were curious, which is part of being a magical being and a child. But believe it or not, we old magicals—we know a thing or two about how to keep you guys safe. Now, does someone want to explain to me why you look like you have been battling Kilomeas in a swamp?"

Everyone glanced at each other, but they quickly put their heads back down. They couldn't tell the headmistress they had gotten in a battle with a bunch of wizards and been saved by Willen. It would sound insane, and would give her even more for her to yell at them. They had gotten themselves in over their heads; they knew that, but what was done was done. Izzie had a lot of questions from that encounter, including how the hell she could fight like that. If her memories were correct, she wouldn't have been battling magical beings on a regular basis at her human orphanage.

Alison took a deep breath and looked at Ms. Berens, tired of the torture of waiting. She just wanted it to be over with.

"It's my fault. I talked them into going. They thought it was a bad idea from the beginning."

Ms. Berens smiled. "Though I appreciate your loyalty to your friends, we both know that is not entirely true. If they had thought it was a bad idea, they would have stayed behind. Speaking of staying behind, please tell me poor Aya chose wisely and is not stuck in the underground city."

"She stayed behind."

"Good." The headmistress pushed up the sleeves of her cloak and sat down in her chair. "Is there anything else that you would like to tell me before I hand down your punishment?"

Alison looked at Izzie, Kathleen, Emma, Luke, Peter, and Ethan, none of whom said a word. She turned back to Ms. Berens and shook her head, knowing she had to keep the upperclassmen's secret. It wasn't *their* fault that the group had gotten caught, and telling the headmistress would only unleash their wrath on the group. She didn't want to spend the rest of her school year running from Scarlett and her cronies. She knew she could take it, but she couldn't even imagine what they would do to poor Emma if they cornered her.

"All right." Ms. Berens let out a deep breath. "Girls, you are going to help tend the magical plants with Professor Fowler. You will report to her tomorrow. It's Sunday, so I will alert her that you will be coming. Boys, you will have library duty under the command of Mr. Decker."

"Oh, God!" Ethan's face dropped. "Are you sure you don't want to expel me?"

The headmistress ignored him and stood. "I want to impress on you that I *should* be expelling every single one of you. This is a serious situation, and you cannot do it again. The underground city can be a very dangerous place if you do not know how to protect yourself, and I have a feeling you got a taste of that tonight. Anyway, I want all of you to go straight to your dorms, clean up, and stay there until the caretaker comes to get you in the morning."

They turned to leave. "Oh, and Izzie and Alison—please stay behind."

The others threw the girls a glance and filed out of the office. Ms. Berens closed the office door and glared at the two of them.

"Alison, I would think after everything you have been through that you of all people would know not to mess with dark magic. That city is *full* of dark magic and you walked straight into it, leading those with no magical training into a dangerous situation. You have *got* to be more responsible."

"Yes, ma'am."

"And you, Izzie! I expected so much more from you."

"How do I know magic?"

"You are an elf, so it's natural."

"But I..."

The headmistress put up her hand. "I don't want to hear another word about it. Consider yourselves lucky you both are still here and not being sent away. I know something else happened down there tonight, but none of you are budging. Whatever it was, I hope you learned your lesson. Now, back to your rooms. I will see you in the plant building bright and early."

Izzie bit her tongue and followed Alison out into the hallway. She waited for the door to shut behind her before letting out a low growl. Alison looked at her, confused.

"You *wanted* to be suspended?"

"No, I *want* to know the truth about my past. When I got here I didn't think I knew anymore magic than how to tie your shoe, but all of a sudden I am a Kung Fu fighting ninja-elf? Yeah, right. I knew there was something missing, something I couldn't quite put my finger on, and I still have no idea what it is."

"That has to be frustrating, but I think right now we just need to get through the punishment and wait for the headmistress to not want to lock us up in the dungeons, and then you can approach her about it. One step at a time, right?"

"I guess so."

The girls walked in silence the rest of the way, went inside, and sat down on their beds. Kathleen looked at the others and pulled her knees to her chin.

"I mean, it could have been much worse. We could have died down there. Or we could have been expelled. I guess playing with some singing flowers isn't all that bad, even if it's going to mess up my manicure."

Emma shook her head. "I'm just glad she didn't call my parents."

The door opened and Aya rushed in, stopping and frowning at them. "Gosh, what happened to you guys?"

"Which part? Getting caught, or fighting three very angry dark wizards?" Izzie half-smiled.

"I don't think I want to know. Did you get expelled?"

Kathleen sighed. "No, just have to work in the flower building with Mrs. Fowler for the next thousand years."

"I was just in there. It's fun! She got in a new set of dragon-eaters."

Kathleen's face dropped. "Whatever that is, I'm keeping my fingers away from it."

"Probably a good idea."

Alison went to the drawer and pulled the gold-speckled egg out, which for some reason felt heavier than before. She sat down on the bed with it in her lap.

"Thanks for having my back during the fight."

"Are you kidding?" Kathleen chuckled. "You and Izzie were the only ones keeping us alive. Then there was the rabid dog, who I now have a lot more respect for. Did you see his teeth?"

"He was pretty badass tonight," Alison smirked. "And Izzie was too, but she needs help to develop her skills…and we are going to help her."

Izzie looked at the girls in surprise. "Really?"

"Hell, yeah.." Kathleen pumped her fist.

"I'm down." Emma nodded.

"I already missed too much excitement." Aya laughed. "I'm in for anything at this point."

Izzie smiled. "Thank you. From what I remember of my past, I've never had any real friends before."

Alison gave her a half-smile. "Well, as long as the upperclassmen don't kill us, we will always have your back."

Just then someone pounded on the door. Izzie looked over and rolled her eyes.

"Speak of the devils and they shall appear."

The presence of the upperclassmen made Izzie cringe. The last thing she wanted to do after the kind of day they'd had was deal with Scarlett and her cronies again.

Aya looked at everyone, raising an eyebrow. She hadn't been there, nor did she understand the gravity of the situation. "Why are the upperclassman pounding on our door?"

Izzie groaned and got off her bed. "Because we saw them coming from the dark area of the city."

"Then you have to tell the headmistress immediately! That's forbidden."

"We understand that, but we were in the wrong too and made a deal that if they didn't tell on us *and* they left us alone for the rest of the year, we would keep their secret."

"But Ms. Berens found out you were there anyway."

"Doesn't mean we break *our* promise."

Kathleen opened one of her bags and pulled out a top, holding it up in front of her. "Imagine what they would do to us if we went back on our word. I don't need that kind of drama in my life."

Izzie shook her head. "Me either."

Someone beat on the door again, this time almost rattling the pictures off the walls. Aya headed for the door, then turned back and stared at Alison.

"What?" Alison looked down at the egg. "Oh. Sorry about that."

She stood and carefully set the speckled egg back in her drawer, pulling the socks and undies around it again. She closed the drawer and wiped the gold and black dust from her hands before nodding, and Aya had just started to open the door when she stumbled backward as Scarlett, Claire, and the gang pushed their way into the room, shutting the door behind them. Scarlett looked around the room, her eyes briefly lingering on the dolls in the corner.

"So, first we want to say that we had nothing to do with you guys getting caught. You apparently were too stupid to wipe away your magical trail before you went into the kemana."

Izzie kicked at the bedpost with the tip of her shoe. "Yeah, just like the trail of dark magic you left leaving the kemana. Good thing Horace is a human and couldn't see it."

Claire's eyes grew wide. "Damn it, Scarlett. I thought you took care of everything."

"I did, but things changed, and we were in a hurry."

Alison walked forward, crossing her arms over her chest as she studied the panic clouding Claire and the other's energy. "What did you come here for? To tell us it wasn't you?"

Scarlett gritted her teeth, clenching her fist. "No, I came here to find out whether you plan on keeping our deal, even though we weren't the ones who told on you."

"A deal's a deal. As long as you hold up the other part of yours."

"It's already been spread around to leave you alone and if you have any issue with anyone you come to me and I'll take care of them."

"Then yes, the deal is still on."

"It'd better be. If you let it slip we'll come down on you so hard you'll spend the rest of this year black and blue." Scarlett turned quickly, pointing at Aya. "And that goes for you too. I know you know what's going on."

Aya nodded, her cheeks red and her hands shaking slightly. Scarlett turned her attention back to Alison, her face softening. "So, what was the punishment?"

Izzie scoffed. "Flower duty with Fowler, and the boys are in the library."

"Ooh." The group winced. "The boys got the crap end of that one."

Alison looked at the others and cleared her throat. "Why were you in the dark area anyway?"

Scarlett's face contorted with anger. "That's none of your damn business. Just remember the deal."

Scarlett turned to leave and the group followed her as she threw open the door and stomped out. The people in the common area scurried back, peeking into the girls' room before Aya slammed the door shut. She turned, her face peaked, looking at Alison and the rest. Whatever was going on with Scarlett and her group, it wasn't anything good.

As promised, the next morning before the sun came up Horace knocked on the door. The girls had known to expect it, so they were dressed and ready to go. Alison answered it and nodded at Horace, who stood to the side to let the girls pass. They went to the dining hall first, where each was given a bowl of cereal and a cup of juice. There wasn't anything magical about the plain yellow box sitting in the center of the table.

"So *this* is what prison is like." Kathleen rolled her eyes and took a bite of her cereal.

Emma giggled. "I imagine it's not quite as comfy."

"And no glass juice cups," Izzie added.

When they were done with breakfast they trudged down to the gardening complex with its three massive greenhouses and fields of plants. Mrs. Fowler was there, her bright red frizzy hair completely untamed, wearing a pair of patchwork gardening pants, a bright pink top, and gardening gloves. She looked up at the girls as they walked through the doors and stared around at all the tools.

"Good morning, ladies. So happy to have some weekend help. The flowers don't take them off, that's for sure." She giggled in a high pitch. "Now, who of you likes vegetables?"

Kathleen timidly raised her hand, staring at Emma. With a sigh Emma raised hers as well, knowing full well she would never hear the end if she didn't. Mrs. Fowler clapped her hands and went to the rows of tools, where she picked up a small hand trowel, a pair of pruning scissors, and two baskets. She handed the tools to Kathleen and the baskets to Emma.

"I am going to make a delicious turnip-green salad tonight, so I need you ladies to walk down the pathway to plot six. You will see signs for the turnips and the radishes. Now, turnips are easy—you simply snip bunches right below the green part and throw them in the basket. The radishes are a bit more work. You need to grab them below the green leaves and pull straight up out of the ground. Then you snip any root that is deeply buried if it doesn't release and toss it in the basket. I need both baskets filled to the top. You think you got that?"

"Yes, ma'am," Emma mumbled.

"Good. Now go on, and watch that you don't stumble into plot four. They don't like visitors too much, especially if you step on one of them."

Emma looked wearily at Kathleen and they headed out. Horace opened the building's wood-slatted door and held back a grin as the two left the building and went toward the large sign in the distance. Mrs. Fowler turned back to Izzie and Alison, clasping her hands together.

"I have something special for the two of you. My singing plants need a good fertilizer change. Come with me."

Izzie gave Alison a side glance as they followed the peripatetic teacher from the garden building to the first greenhouse. She opened the door and the girls were greeted with the harmonious tones of plants singing the 50s greatest hits in harmony with the music. Izzie bobbed her head and smiled.

"They sing as long as the background music is on. Now,

if the music stops for some reason, they get really angry and will take a finger off if you aren't careful. But that rarely happens."

Alison lifted an eyebrow and Izzie exhaled hard. She glanced at Alison and shrugged.

"At least we get some good music while we work."

Mrs. Fowler giggled. "Depends on what you call 'good music.' *These* singing plants are fine. Today, however, you are going to be working with the rejects."

"The rejects? Do they have bad voices?"

"No, they just like a different kind of music."

Mrs. Fowler gestured for them to follow her and led them into a smaller greenhouse in the back. Alison could hear muffled drums and guitars. Mrs. Fowler stepped to the door and shook her head.

"Hope you like metal."

When she opened the door a wild wind blew the girls' hair straight back and the screams echoed in their ears. Alison clapped her hands over her ears and looked at Mrs. Fowler, who pulled two sets of earplugs out of her gardening apron and handed each girl one. Once the sound was at least muffled she showed them the tools and left them with a smile on her face.

Alison and Izzie took their places across from each other, watching the plants thrash their flowers up and down and use their leaves to play air guitar. Both girls reached forward just as the music stopped, and they quickly pulled back their hands. The plants growled and chomped at the air until the music finally came back on. Alison lifted her eyebrows and looked at Izzie, who sighed and shook her head. What a punishment—left to lose digits to headbanging plants.

They worked without speaking, mostly because the music was so loud they couldn't hear a word anyone said. After each plant had been pruned it would look at them, hold up two leaves, and stick its tongue out of its tiny mouth. They were both starting to think detention in the library would have been a quiet ride compared to that.

Across the fields stood Kathleen, swatting at flies as Emma cut the turnip leaves and handed them to her. She looked over her shoulder at plot four, where rows of tall orange flowers stared at them with beady dark eyes. Their stems and leaves were gnarled and twisted, resembling sharp claws, and Emma was positive she saw one of them flash fangs at her. Along the fence line of plot four were several warnings.

Vampire Flora, STAY BACK.

CERTAIN DEATH.

CAUTION, BLOODSUCKERS.

Kathleen turned to Emma, slightly fearful. "Why do we even preserve plants like that from Oriceran. Let them die out with the planet!"

"You say that about them, yet you could say that about any living creature." Emma pulled hard on a radish in the row next to the turnips, but the stems slipped from her hands. She fell back into the bushes and her hand landed in a pile of manure. "Yuck."

The girls worked all day, pausing once for sandwiches Horace brought over. When they were done the four of them headed back up to the dorms, utterly exhausted. On the chair outside the showers was a basket with towels and soaps and a note from Aya.

"Figured you would need these before coming back to the room. Burn your clothes."

Alison chuckled as Kathleen read the note aloud. "Seems like she is finally getting a sense of humor."

Emma sniffed her collar and winced. "Or maybe she was serious."

The girls cleaned up and headed to their rooms to change for Sunday dinner. Aya wasn't in the room; she was still studying. There was a box with several different postage stamps sitting on Alison's bed. Her name and the address of the school were written sloppily on the label with Braille printed under each line. She knew immediately it had to be from Brownstone and Shay. She hastily opened the box and started pulling things out, grabbing the attention of the other girls.

"Those clothes are boring but cute. Just your style." Kathleen yawned.

Alison held up several plain t-shirts, cute cargo pants—which obviously had been purchased by Shay—and a bright red shirt with umbrellas on it which was probably Brownstone's doing. She smiled and put the clothes to the side. There were also new satin undies, two boxes of tampons, some Midol, a few bags of snacks, some lip gloss, and a vanilla-scented body spray—everything Shay would think a girl needed. In the bottom was a note in Braille from Brownstone. She pulled it out and unfolded it, feeling dirt clinging to the edges.

Alison,

Thought you might need this stuff. Shay and I are proud of you for doing so well, and we hope you are starting to feel at home. Ms. Berens says you are doing fantastic. We will see you at Christmas Break.

Take Care.

James

P.S. The umbrella shirt was from me."

Alison smiled as she folded the letter back up and stuck it in her drawer. She folded her new clothes, feeling a little less alone in the world, and set the red umbrella shirt to the side. It was hideous, but she didn't just want to throw it away. Maybe Peter would like it. He was strange enough to wear it proudly.

The girls spent the rest of the evening eating dinner and preparing for school the next day. They didn't know if their punishment was over or if it would bleed into their other weekends, but they were happy to have today done and over with. Alison and the rest would definitely think twice before breaking that rule again...

They never knew what would happen in the future, though.

Izzie leaned back in her chair as she waited for class to start. Everyone was chatting about their weekends. Peter had escaped from detention in the library. Izzie noticed his eyebrow had a new section missing, which led her to believe he had spent his weekend playing with some sort of science-magic concoction—and not to a positive end. Ethan was sitting in the seat against the wall, one foot in his chair, whittling another wood-working project. He rarely paid any attention to the other students, unless of course there was some kind of drama to take in. The girls were seated all around Izzie, and Emma and Kathleen were telling the others about the "terrifying Vampire Plants." Aya studying as usual as Alison flipped through the pages of her Dark Energy textbook, one hand feeling the passing raised dots. She seemed to be frantic to find something.

"Alison, what in the world are you looking for?"

"Drow."

"I don't think they hide out in high school textbooks."

"No, but information on them might. I found info a while ago in an old book at the library. I figured why not check in this one?"

"But that's a Dark Energy text..."

Alison immediately stopped flipping the pages and closed the book, giving Izzie a forced smile. "You're right. Didn't think about that."

Alison let out a slow deep breath. She didn't want her friends to think she was some sort of dark magical being hell-bent on destroying Earth, and that was what everyone made a Drow sound like. She was relieved when the professor walked into the room, ending any questions that Izzie might have asked. Maybe it was better to keep whatever information she found to herself, at least until she figured out the truth.

Professor Xander Powell had been teaching the freshmen about dark energy in magic. He was a very intelligent man who rarely smiled, but Alison could see the kindness in his soul. He wore a perfectly-pressed dark blue suit every single day, and his hair was peppered white and grey with a matching beard. He was serious about the dangers of dark magic, and made sure not to make it sound fun or flashy in any of his lectures. From the swirl of dark energy that moved around him, Alison could tell he'd had his own run-ins with dark magic.

"All right, class, settle down. Ethan, put the wood away."

"Yeah, Ethan, put your wood away," one of the other students shouted, bringing a low roar of laughter from everyone else.

Ethan showed the kid the middle finger and shoved his stuff into his bag. Mr. Powell sighed and took off his glasses, rubbing them with his handkerchief. He put them back on and blinked a couple of times before opening his notes.

"In this class we have gone over several things, including the dark mist, the World in Between, and the use of dark magic in historically positive respects. Today we are going to continue the theme and discuss the history of one of the most well-known dark wizards in history, one who only recently died. Who knows who I am speaking of? Alison?"

Alison cringed and cleared her throat. "Rhazdon, Professor Powell."

"Exactly! Rhazdon, who until recently we believed to be a wizard, but it turned out she was half-Atlantean. This history lesson will be a long one, mostly because through dark magic Rhazdon was able to live for over eight hundred years.

"Rhazdon was born and raised on Earth, a normal magical being like any other child...or so we thought. Rhazdon not only was exceptionally capable in both potions and artifact magic, but she was a very powerful natural witch."

Izzie had never heard Rhazdon's name before, but there was something in the back of her mind that made the story very familiar. There wasn't a magical being on Earth or in Oriceran who didn't know Rhazdon's story, or at least how much of a threat she had been with the uprising of magical beings, but Izzie was still struggling. Her mind was constantly fuzzy; some things familiar, others not.

"Rhazdon and her followers were misguided. But in the end she was remorseful for what she had unleashed onto the worlds and as her last act tried to make things right. Eight hundred and twenty years ago when a war raged between the Followers and many of our own, people died or were damned to the World in Between, and lives were changed forever. Does anyone know who sparked the rise of Rhazdon? Yes, Ethan?"

"The seer shared the theory that when the next Golden Age comes it will drain the last of Oriceran's magic and all creatures must go to Earth or perish."

"Very good." Xander was impressed. Ethan wasn't the kind of student to answer questions freely.

"*But*," Ethan added loudly. "That wasn't why I raised my hand."

Xander sighed. "Okay, why did you?"

"I have a question. It's a bit off topic, but Rhazdon's history isn't changing so I figured it would be okay."

Xander just stared at Ethan, who swallowed hard and glanced at Peter.

"I was wondering if you could maybe take a break and talk to us about the dark magic that happens in the underground cities."

"Yeah," one of the other students called. "We should know these things in case we need to protect ourselves."

"The only reason you would need to protect yourself was if you were wandering through an undesirable area—and that should *not* be on the top of your list of rules to break."

Alison and the rest of her friends all looked at each other, knowing that was not true. They didn't want to talk about what had happened, but at the same time, if it was something that could help they really couldn't shy away from the truth. Alison took a deep breath and raised her hand, ignoring Ethan's pleading stare.

"Yes, Alison?"

"I want to talk about a hypothetical situation."

"All right, go on."

"Let's say there were a group of students in the underground city, and they were in all the right areas. And let's say they walked up to the edge of the rich area...um... I don't remember what it's called."

"I am assuming you are referring to Opulence."

"Yes, that's it. So, say they go to the edge of Opulence to take in the view, and they are attacked by dark wizards. What would they do then? They weren't in an undesirable area and they weren't doing anything wrong, but they found themselves in a bad situation."

Xander cleaned his glasses again and looked at Alison, not with concern, but more with knowledge. He cleared his throat and sat down at his desk. He didn't want to have this discussion, but it never failed that something about the underground city's dark magic always came up. After all, he *was* the Dark Energy teacher, and got questions about it constantly in his upper-level classes.

"In this underground city and all the other ones, there are undesirable parts of town. Dark magic has been a draw for magical beings since the beginning of time. Think about what you know about humans: they try to live wholesome lives, but they are constantly drawn to their dark sides. Drinking, drugs, murder, anger, rage—they are all forms of dark energy. Even the best of the humans can fall victim to their temptations. Dark magic is no different."

Ethan raised his hand again but didn't wait to be called on. "But what *kind* of dark magic?"

"Every kind," Xander stated bluntly, leaning forward. "The dark areas of our underground cities are crawling with people like Rhazdon, those who crave the dark magic and have given their souls to it in exchange for worldly pleasures. The magic can turn on them at any time, and works through every living creature. There are potions that will turn the kindest magical being into a bloodthirsty beast. There are poisons, spells, and mind control. There are those who would strike you dead with a forbidden curse and never blink an eye. There are creatures we thought long lost even on Oriceran that slink through the shadows, even royalty that has long since been forgotten."

Alison shifted in her seat uncomfortably, thinking about her mother, about the pictures in the book from the library. She thought about what Brownstone had told her about her mother, about how her mother had been a two hundred and twelve-year-old Drow princess—strong and powerful—but that was the extent of what he knew. That technically made *Alison* a princess, but when she had been told she had pushed it out of her mind, not wanting to be any different than her classmates. However, since the tides were changing and after what had happened in the dark city with the wizards, she couldn't help but revisit it. Maybe her being some sort of ancient royalty had some-thing to do with the attack?

"It has always been known that light is attracted to dark. They pull and push against each other and one cannot survive without the other. What is less talked about is..." The professor stopped pacing and stood in front of

Alison's desk, looking down at her, "dark is almost *always* attracted to dark. Maybe those kids should ask themselves why they attracted the dark wizards? They don't come out for just anything."

Alison looked into Mr. Powell's dark brown eyes and he held her glance for several moments. Over the loudspeaker the bell rang, breaking their eye contact. Alison breathed heavily, looking from side to side trying to figure out just how Mr. Powell knew what she had been thinking. It was impossible, right? He had to have just read into it, since there wasn't a professor at the school who didn't know Alison was a Drow now.

Izzie nudged Alison and glanced at Mr. Powell. "Come on, we have study hall in the library."

"Right." Alison shook her head and grabbed her books, looking back at Mr. Powell, whose eyes followed her curiously until she was out the doors. She turned the corner to find the group waiting for her, and Ethan grabbed her arm and pulled her out into the courtyard.

"*Why would you ask something like that?* Did you see the way everyone looked at us? They knew we had done something we weren't supposed to."

"I needed to know why those wizards attacked out of nowhere. Why they picked *us.*"

"Uh, because we were six lowerclassmen wandering around the underground city all alone on the edge of Opulence? They saw easy targets."

"No." Alison pulled her arm away and shook her head. "They weren't trying to bully us or scare us, they were trying to kill us. The magic they were using—I've seen it before."

"It was dark magic."

"Yes, but they used it like grown wizards and witches would. They were sent there; I know it. And when they returned losers, the sky darkened. It was a sign from whoever sent them out there for us."

Izzie put her hand on Alison's shoulder. "Maybe you are just upset and overthinking all this. What would they want with all of us? Why would anyone go out of their way to kill some weird magical kids and two orphans?"

"They weren't sent out for all of us, just me."

"Alison, I appreciate you being a martyr, but I don't think that's the case."

"It most likely is." Luke walked up to the group. "I could sense their intentions, and they were zeroed in on Alison. It didn't make any sense, but that's what it was. If they had wanted you guys dead they would have killed you. You don't know enough magic. The only ones giving them a hard time were Izzie and Alison."

Ethan took a deep breath and tapped his chin, thinking. "Okay, and why would they want to kill you?"

"I don't know, maybe because I'm a Drow?" Alison knew there was more to it than that, but she wasn't about to blab her secret to everyone. It was not only irresponsible at that point, it was dangerous, and she didn't even know enough about it to explain.

"I know Drow aren't the most popular beings on the planet, but to provoke a battle for no reason seems a bit out there."

The bell rang again, signaling that they were late for study hall. Ethan shook his head and threw his bag over his shoulder. "Come on, we don't need to be any later. Detention yesterday was enough for one week."

Izzie smiled and twined her arm through Alison's. They headed toward the library slowly, not saying a word to each other. Alison liked that about Izzie; she didn't have to spill all her secrets and thoughts. She was just there no matter what, kind of like during the fight. Alison let the thoughts rampage through her mind, wondering if there was any truth to her theory. If there wasn't, great, but if there was they could be facing a real threat—all because of her heritage. It was just another instance of something happening that Alison couldn't control, only this time she was afraid that it could get her friends killed.

When the girls were fast asleep that night, Izzie opened her eyes and carefully slipped out of bed. She pulled her jeans on slowly and quietly and drew her hoodie over her head. Sleeping just wasn't ever in the cards for her, and she'd gotten into the habit of wandering the grounds. It was the only time she could think without the hustle and bustle of everyone around them. It wasn't the perfect scenario, but she was at least left alone with her thoughts every once in a while.

She sat down on the edge of her bed and pulled on her shoes, then stood up carefully, pausing as Kathleen grumbled and rolled over.

"Where are you headed?" Alison was sitting up in bed, already throwing back the covers.

"Nowhere… go back to sleep."

"I'm coming with you. You could use the company." Alison could see the pain radiating through Izzie's soul. She was lonely, but for something she couldn't understand.

Izzie grabbed her satchel and pulled it over her head and across her chest as Alison pulled on her jeans and slipped on her shoes.

"I can't talk you out of it? We could get caught, you know."

"I'm coming."

"Suit yourself," Izzie whispered, annoyed and grateful at the same time. She took a look around the room one more time and headed out the door, closing it carefully behind them.

Students were technically not supposed to roam the mansion late at night, but there were a number of upper-classmen boys that went to the dining hall for a late-night snack. No one would pay a bit of attention to them.

When they reached the bottom of the stairs they ducked behind the staircase for a moment, letting a group of three boys walk into the dining hall. They scooted through the lobby and out the front doors, heading quickly across the lawn and out into the pastures. Once out of sight of the front steps Izzie pushed her hood back, letting the cool breeze blow her hair around. She closed her eyes and took in a deep breath of fresh air, listening to the frogs and crickets in the background. They would be gone soon with the weather changing, and she would miss it. Alison looked around at the calm energy emanating from the woods.

They moved through the tall grass and climbed to the top of the hill, as Izzie looked in all directions to find Horace. "You have to promise not to tell the others, Alison."

"I give you my word."

Horace was usually out that time of night doing his

rounds with the dogs, and she often kept him company on his walks. Izzie didn't see any sign of him though, and his tiny cottage on the outskirts of the teachers' housing area was dark.

Izzie shrugged, figuring he was busy sleeping instead of worrying about idiot students like her who decided to go wandering around the place. "We should head back," she said to Alison.

"You lookin' for me?" Horace called from behind her. "I see you brought a friend this time. Good for you."

"Hey." Izzie turned around, smiling sheepishly. "Alison couldn't sleep either. We went out for a night stroll and figured I'd catch up with you if you were out here. Thought maybe you had called it a night."

"And let students get carried off by gargoyles? Nah, as much as that appeals to me for some of them, I'd be a terrible caretaker if I let that happen."

Izzie laughed. "Depends on which ones. So, where you headed to tonight?"

"Figured I'd head over to the orchard. Some of the older boys like to sneak out there with their girlfriends. I usually just scare the crap out of them and watch them run off, pants around their ankles, but it's pretty late in the season so it will surprise me if we find anyone."

"I kind of hope not." Alison grimaced.

"Mind if we walk with you?" asked Izzie.

"Not at all." Horace handed Izzie one of the dogs' leashes and they set off toward the back side of the property. There were all kinds of fruit trees planted out there, some from Earth and others from Oriceran. They tried to keep them separate, unsure what would happen if they cross-pollinated. No one wanted a peach with teeth.

"You can't sleep either, huh?" He smiled at Alison

"No." She groaned. Lately it had been getting worse. The truth was she had seen Izzie leaving late at night before and thought Izzie could use the company.

Izzie gave her a reluctant smile as the dog pulled on the leash. "I thought it was just me."

Alison brushed a strand of hair out of her face. "I don't know what it is. I mean, I don't *feel* like I've been up for weeks. I feel fine. But I can't fall asleep."

"Let me ask you a question. Do you ever zone out, like go into some sort of trance state? You can hear around you, but you are in a haze, your body relaxed, your mind blocking the constant chatter?"

Alison frowned. "Actually, yeah. At least once a day, usually after school on my bed. Emma thinks I meditate so they just kind of leave me alone."

"If someone touches you, do you come to kind of like you've been woken from a deep sleep?"

"Yes! Oh my God, yes. What is that?"

"I did some research last time I was in the underground city. Figured you would want to know a little more about your people. I came across a section on sleep and it said that Drow generally do not sleep, not like most creatures anyway. They go into a trance-like state where their bodies rejuvenate. They were so busy underground all the time that taking some time to stop and trance out every once in a while throughout the day was easiest for them. So, I guess you not sleeping is a Drow thing."

"That's crazy…" She shook her head. "I don't sleep, I make purple flames, and I go into trances."

"There's a lot more to the Drow, and I think over time you'll notice more and more powers developing. Your appearance will change too."

Izzie looked at Alison and felt herself relaxing. *I'm not the only one who's different.*

"Yeah, Brownstone told me that. He said my skin will darken and my hair will probably turn completely silver like my mother's. I never thought there could actually be freaks in the magical world, but here I am."

"You think that too?" Izzie blurted out the words.

"You're not a freak. Neither one of you are," he chuckled. "I grew up a bright red head in Austin Texas. They called me a freak all the time, but I think there it's more of a compliment. Strange place."

"That's right, you grew up in Texas, I forgot. What's it like?" Izzie scratched the dog behind his ears.

"Big and beautiful." He laughed. "My parents worked at the mill outside of town and had a small farm, which is why I knew how to take care of property like this one."

"But as a human, how did you fall in with the magical folks?"

"My Aunt Estelle owns a bar in Austin, she has all kinds of folks coming in and out of there. She hooked me up, guess she got in good with them. Actually, the headmistress knows my aunt too. Her granddaughter, Leira, used to live behind the bar my aunt owned. She was a detective, never knew she was magical, then one day her whole world changed. She's actually speaking next week here at the school, you'll hear all about her then."

"Oh, that's right, special guest speaker Leira Berens. She's a bounty hunter now, right? Wasn't she the one who helped take down Rhazdon?"

"Yeah, her and a whole slew of others. But in the end, Rhazdon gave her life to help others. Complicated woman."

"I think I heard Brownstone and Shay talk about her once." Horace put out his hand and helped Alison down the steep embankment as Izzie easily ran ahead, waiting at the bottom.

"Living in Texas taught me a lot of things, and so did my aunt. She is a pistol, doesn't take crap from no one. I can always count on her being right there behind her bar, cleaning something, a cigarette hanging off her lip, her hair in a tall bouffant just like it's been since before I was born. I'm glad she recommended me for this job. I really like being here. I've made a lot of good friends, met a lot of good people along the way."

"I'm sure your fair share of bad ones too."

"That's for sure."

They walked to the edge of the orchard and looked out across the fields of trees. Alison let out a deep breath and smiled, seeing small wisps of magical energy dancing through them. She stepped closer narrowing her eyes, realizing that there was so much she was missing during the normal hustle and bustle of the days. There were so many people all the souls started to just meld together, but at night she could see all the little details she normally overlooked.

"There are magical creatures out there."

"You see a lot more than I do," whispered Izzie, reaching out to squeeze Alison's hand.

"I see a lot of different things."

"Yep," said Horace. "There are small magical creatures all over these hills. They are the fairies and tree gnomes. They live here under our protection, but they stay in the background, living their lives just like anyone else. They like to be close to the kemana. In fact, I've heard rumors that there are a few of those crazy furry trolls roaming around here somewhere too. But don't go chasing them. Ms. Berens said her granddaughter saved one's life one time and now he's bonded to her for life. They are like tiny hairy little Yodas."

"Interesting." Izzie chuckled. "I'll make sure to walk the other way if I see one."

"Their souls are orange and green," said Horace.

Alison turned her head looking at Horace with surprise. "You know about me? Did Ms. Berens tell you?"

"Eventually but I'd already figured it out. You don't see the details like everyone else does, and the way you study each and every person… I knew you were seeing them in a different way than the rest of us."

"Guess I can add that to the list of weird things about me."

"Not weird, just different, and different can be really good. For example, what do you see when you look at this section right here?"

"I see fairies and… there." Alison pointed about half way down the closest orchard. "Two elves, desire circulating their energies."

"You mean making out?" Izzie laughed, clamping her hand over her mouth.

"See? I would have probably completely missed them. All I see is trees."

Horace turned to walk back up the hill and the girls followed as Alison looked back at the energy "Aren't you gonna stop them?"

"Eh, I'm feeling generous tonight. Who am I to stand in the way of love?"

Alison laughed and reached up, taking his hand as she climbed the embankment behind Izzie. "Can we take the dogs through the pastures?" asked Alison.

"Sure, why not," said Izzie, running ahead, making a loop and coming back to them. It was better being out at night with a friend. *A friend.*

Alison looked out over the fields, noticing the souls she normally missed. She felt like she was seeing everything for the first time, her wonderment lifted her spirits. It had been a long time since she felt that way—curious, excited, filled with a warm glow. She didn't even think about everything that had happened while she wandered. It opened her senses, something she had needed to do for a long time.

When the sun was just starting to brighten the sky, Horace walked the two girls back to the mansion. Izzie stood there looking out over the frosty morning grasses, her hands shoved in her pockets to keep them warm. She gave Horace a hug, surprising him. He chuckled and hugged her back.

"Just remember, when things get overwhelming and overbearing for either one of you, there are always creatures out there for you to discover, to watch dance through the forest at night. You don't ever have to feel alone. Us freaks, we stick together."

Alison and Izzie laughed, taking each other's hand as they climbed the steps to the dorms. They went to their room and Izzie sat down on the edge of her bed. The alarms hadn't gone off yet, and the whole mansion was still silent. She stared out the window watching the sunrise and wondered how long she could keep that feeling. A friend.

She knew a lot was going on, just like she knew there was a lot more to her and her past than she really understood, but it was nice to spend one night just acting like a normal teenager. She almost felt like with the sun rose the problems, but without it, nothing would grow.

"You're back," Emma whispered from her bed. "I heard you leave last night and I was a bit worried."

Alison smiled. "Thanks, but I'm okay. Just don't sleep very much, so I went for walk down to the orchards." She kept her word and didn't mention anything about Izzie.

"Are they beautiful? I haven't been yet."

"They are the prettiest thing I have seen here yet, except for maybe the Vampire Flowers of course."

Emma covered her mouth and giggled as Alison grabbed her things and headed to the showers. She was ready to start a new day, to try to figure out who she was, and in the moments between, just enjoy being there. She knew times wouldn't stay that simple for long, not with royal Drow blood flowing through her. Dark days were just over the horizon. Alison had a sneaking suspicion they weren't going to wait for her to be ready, to know who she was and to prepare for the worst. Until then, she had the orchards and her friends, two things that she could never turn her back on, that was for sure.

Alison sat in the quiet of the library, her hands resting on her potions book. They had midterms coming up in about a month, and she wanted to make sure she passed with flying colors. She was tired, and she had not gone into a trance for the past day. Her evenings were spent walking the grounds with Izzie, gazing at the different souls flickering and flashing across the grounds. It was now their quiet time. Little moments carved out of each day where they forgot about all the stressful stuff like tests and grades and just focused on the world around them. The only grownup they ever saw out there was Horace. He didn't pepper them with questions —he just talked, leaving space if they wanted to interject.

"Hey." Emma slid into the seat next to her and looked around the room for Leo.

"Hey. He's in the vault. What's up?"

"The assembly is starting. I figured you would want to come."

"It's mandatory, isn't it?"

"Yeah." Emma giggled. "Grab Izzie and meet us there."

"Gotcha."

Alison sighed and returned her books to the shelf. The librarian poked his head out and stared at Alison, nodding as she gave him a sloppy salute. The flower in his hat actually smiled for once, instead of blowing the normal raspberries. Alison finished cleaning up and headed up to their room, poking her head in to find Izzie lying across the bed reading a book.

"Hey, the assembly is starting."

"Yay." Izzie rolled her eyes. "So excited to hear about someone else's perfect life."

"Not sure it was perfect."

"Maybe wasn't, but is now."

"Oh, come on." Alison smiled. "We gotta go. It's mandatory, remember?"

"How could I forget?" Izzie rolled out of the bed and slipped her shoes on. "Ms. Berens reminded me like a hundred times."

"Oh yeah, this is Ms. Berens' granddaughter. Totally forgot."

Over the months Izzie had sunk deeper and deeper into her thoughts, trying to pull out the things she couldn't remember. Everyone just wrote her off as a typical brooding teenager, but for her it was more than hormones. She wanted to know why her mind was so fuzzy, why she didn't have the typical memories everyone else had, and if she did they just sprang out of nowhere like they had escaped a trap. For the last two weeks, she'd been having dreams with the same sweet and even-toned woman's voice telling her over and over how proud she was of her. It was getting to be more than a little frustrating for her, but Ms. Berens just brushed her off anytime she brought up the subject.

She shuffled her feet along the floor and Alison smiled and put her arm around her shoulder. The two girls walked down to the bottom floor, then took a left and entered the auditorium. The place was packed, and everyone else was super excited to listen to Leira's story. This was the woman who had lived most of her life as a human and then suddenly learned she was a Jasper Elf, a race that was virtually extinct both on Earth and Oriceran. Everything after that had been dark-magic-kicking Rhaz-don-smacking elf-loving history. She had become a legend in the magical community.

Alison and Izzie squeezed down one of the rows to the two seats Emma had saved for them. Kathleen looked excited and Peter had a picture of Leira in his lap, hoping to get an autograph. Izzie rolled her eyes and sat back.

"I don't understand. She's like a celebrity, but damn... she's *just* a cop."

Alison elbowed her and gave her a sideways glance and the two elves in front of them turned around and shot Izzie menacing glares. The lights dimmed, and the head-mistress walked onto the stage to a rousing welcome by the students. She pushed a piece of her long brown hair behind her ear and waved her hands, wearing a small smirk.

"Thank you, everyone, for coming," she began excitedly. "Today's guest is visiting from Washington DC, and was originally from Austin, Texas. She has been a human detective, a civil servant with the United States magical sector, received tutelage under our very own Turner Underwood, and now serves as a freelance agent helping our magical community fit in here on Earth. So, without further ado, I present my granddaughter—*Leira Berens.*"

Izzie sat up a bit as Leira walked onto the stage. She had the same dark hair as the headmistress, but hers was pulled back in a tight ponytail. She was wearing a white button-down shirt, black dress pants, and flats. Izzie could tell she wasn't used to dressing up, and she looked uncomfortable. Around her wrist was a bracelet that dangled and shimmered in the stage lights. The students cheered and chanted as she approached the microphone.

She stepped up and smiled awkwardly, gazing out at the crowd. She leaned forward to say something into the mic, but it gave a strange hissing sound. Leira flipped the mic off and closed her eyes for a moment, and streams of light moved up her body, and the symbols on her arms and neck began flipping too fast to read. She pulled the energy to her throat, and as the light faded she opened her eyes and smiled at the crowd.

"Did that work?" Her voice was magically amplified. "Good. Thank you, everyone, for such a warm welcome. My grandmother did say there was an amazing group of kids here at this school."

Leira looked around the auditorium, shaking her head in awe. "This is great. I went to a regular human high school, and we didn't have anything like *this.* Just a small auditorium with a few poorly-made stage pieces for the theatre."

She swallowed hard and paused for a moment, and Alison saw that her energy was growing nervous. She had fought some of the most dangerous wizards on both planets and room full of teenagers made her nervous? Alison liked that because it made her more real, but she could see Izzie's irritation. Izzie looked at the edge of the stage where the headmistress was standing with her hands clasped in front of her, pride all but seeping from her skin. Next to her was a furry troll about three feet tall with a tuft of green hair. He was devouring a bag of Cheetos and wiping his now-orange paws down his front.

Leira pulled out a piece of paper and cleared her throat. "So, I was born and raised in Austin, Texas, a place I miss very much. I had my trials as a human, never knowing inside of me was more magic than Harry Potter had."

The crowd let out a laugh. Emma looked at Alison and smiled in awe. "She's so great."

"My mom always talked about Oriceran and the Light Elves—too much at the time, I suppose. She was put into a mental institution for many years, proving just how little the humans knew. The next few years were spent under the care of my grandmother—your headmistress—until her disappearance. Little did I know that my mother was telling the truth and my grandmother was stuck in the World in Between. I worked hard, didn't really make that many friends, and ended up going to school to become a cop. What I *really* wanted was to be a detective, so I busted my ass and finally became one. I took on all kinds of cases in Austin, from murders to robberies. In the meantime I constantly searched for clues that would lead me to my grandmother, but there was no trace."

Alison looked around the room, spotting the soul colors of Claire and Scarlett sitting on the edge of their seats, completely enthralled by Leira's story. So far Alison could imagine her trials, giving her the sense that Leira too had always felt like she didn't belong.

"One day I started to see funny things around me and I thought, 'Well, hell, I'm going crazy just like my mother.' That was when the Light Elves jumped through a portal into my tiny living room—the day that changed my life. I was hired to do a job for the Queen of the Light Elves, and that turned into a much bigger thing. My magic started to sprout, and kept growing until finally they realized I was no normal elf. I was a Jasper Elf, one with special human DNA. Do I think of myself as special? No." She chuckled. "But I did find that between my magical abilities and my human instincts I made one *hell* of a detective."

Everyone clapped and cheered as the furry troll ran onto the stage to bring Leira a bottle of water. She tousled his green hair and he hurried back to the headmistress.

The crowd got quiet again.

"You see, as a human, I never felt like I fit in, not unless I was chasing a perp down the street. And as a Jasper Elf, it was worse. None of the magical folks wanted to be near me, and the humans just didn't understand. I was stuck between again, somewhere I really was tired of being. As time went by I used my strengths as a cop to run down some of the worst dark magic creatures out there, including Rhazdon, all while trying to understand this extremely powerful gift of magic that was apparently trying to take me out."

The crowd laughed. Jasper Elves were special; they harnessed the true energy of pure white light. Legend said that they became so engrossed in the peace of the light they allowed themselves to be enveloped by it, leaving the world behind. Alison looked at Izzie, who covered her mouth as she yawned.

"I decided to combine my experience as a cop and my new magic to help both the magical community and my home planet. I worked with many amazing people, but in the end decided to go out on my own, taking assignments with whatever organization needed me the most. Now don't be fooled: this is not the end of my story. This has come with heartache, loss, stress, and near-death experiences. It has been a struggle to find my place in both worlds, but I know that if I can do it, then you can too. You have to learn what your strengths are and figure out just where you fit in and can be of service. Sometimes you might even have to create your own place."

Everyone stood to give Leira an ovation. They were in awe of her life and her strength and motivated by her story. Alison stood up slowly and clapped, wondering if she would ever find *her* place. There were big differences between Jasper Elves and Drow, one being they usually fought on different sides. People were always less afraid of the light than they were of the dark, though in reality, both could be equally destructive.

"Thank you, everyone. I just want to add one thing to that story, which is that I didn't do any of it alone. I had help from all over the place. It started with a noble Light Elf, then a fuzzy little troll came into my life, and it went from there. There were humans and magical people all over who lent a hand to help me find my place. So just remember, when you feel lost and like you don't have a place in this world, the people who are there to help will lift you up, whether it's family or friends."

Alison smiled and reached over to take Izzie's hand. She could see Izzie's boredom in her energy, but she could also see the pain in her soul. Izzie gripped back tightly and looked at Alison, shaking her head but not saying a single word. She knew Alison was there for her—and vice versa—but the world was really becoming a lonely place. All she could do was hope it turned around for her and got easier for Alison. They deserved their chance, just as Leira Berens had deserved hers.

When the event was over some of the students went to the front to talk to Leira, but Izzie and Alison made their way to the dining hall to grab some dessert. Neither of them said much; they just enjoyed not being alone and having the space to think clearly. They sat down at their normal table, and a three-tiered chocolate cake appeared in the center.

Alison raised an eyebrow and Izzie shrugged. "Sometimes you just need some sweet with your bitter."

Alison paused, then both girls burst into laughter. That was damn right! Sometimes you *did* need to mix the good with the bad. It was the only way you would still get up every morning and forge ahead. She just hoped Izzie could find that balance too. She needed it badly.

2 7

When the weather started to change to winter, Alison received another box. In it was a carefully-wrapped long black coat with some sort of fur on the inside. Below that was another gift, messily wrapped in comics from the newspaper and tied with a shoestring. Inside was a brightly-colored scarf and a wool hat with a pair of matching gloves. She couldn't help but laugh at the scarf. It was the warmest thing she had ever worn. With it came a note with the familiar raised bumps in Braille.

This was made from some sort of strange animal. An alpaca I believe they said.

Hope you like it.

Brownstone.

She had worn it a couple of times, but it wasn't until that night that it became cold enough to really bundle up. Alison slipped quietly out of her bed and dressed, pulling on her coat, scarf, and hat, and shoving the gloves into her pockets. She looked over at Izzie who was sleeping soundly for once and she thought about nudging her but smiled instead and left her alone.

"Good for you, my friend."

Alison carefully maneuvered down the stairs and out the front door. She didn't even realize how cold it was until she reached the hill and a cold burst of wind whipped across her rosy cheeks. She loved it though, the cold made her feel alive, and she was curious as to what kind of magical creatures would be out in the coming winter night's air.

Alison made her way through the pasture and over to the stables where she saw the light was still on. She carefully pushed open the barn doors, the wind blowing the straw through the air. She shut the door behind her and smiled at Horace who was finishing up grooming one of the horses. He looked up as the dogs raced across the barn, almost knocking Alison off her feet.

"You'd think they would get used to seeing you every night."

"I like the warm welcome."

"Where's your friend?"

Alison smiled at the word, friend. "She was practically snoring. I left her in her warm bed."

"Probably smart. Sounds like the kind of thing friends do for each other." Horace reached over and grabbed a wooden stool, setting it down next to him as he cleaned out the horse's hooves. "Come on have a seat. It's a cold one out there tonight. Wasn't sure if you would make your normal trek. I'm sure if you talked to Ms. Berens she'd let you wander the mansion or even the garden building."

"I like the outside, it doesn't make me feel so pinned in.

Besides, who knows what kinds of plants are in the garden area, I like my limbs where they are."

"Yeah, tell me about it. The Vampire Plants don't like the cold, so I have been building little huts around them. Luckily, they don't like human blood, but it took them a minute to figure that out. I swear I woke up the next morning half expecting to have fangs and sparkly skin."

"You read too many books, I doubt vampires—if there were such a thing—would have sparkly skin."

"Yeah? And when I was a kid I never imagined plants with fangs or flying stone figures either. I'm not ruling anything out at this point."

Alison laughed and reached up, petting the horse as it lowered his head toward her. He was kind with soft brown hair, a streak of white running down his head all the way to the tip of his tail. The kids nicknamed him Skunky, but Alison liked his original name, Lightning. He had a soft soul, a kind one, and it didn't ever spike. There was a little magic in all Earth animals, something Alison found intriguing. Magic right under the human nose and they kept them as pets.

"You should have probably given up on tonight's walk, you have midterms in a couple of weeks. Then it's winter break."

"I've been studying for weeks. Ever since Leira Berens came. Her story is inspiring, and she's done a lot for the Earth magical community, I just have a hard time connecting with it. She is pure light, a lot easier for people to be at ease around. Drow are known for being dark creatures."

"You gotta stop reading those books and just go on

your own journey. A being is not predisposed to be light or dark, they choose that path. Magic doesn't force itself on anyone, you have to choose whether you want to give into the pull of the darkness or fight for the light. At least that's how Ms. Berens explained it to me, just like humans and their vices. They choose to give into the dark, it's a hell of a lot easier than searching out the light sometimes, that's for sure. All creatures, human and magical alike have similar struggles, you just gotta remember we are all living, breathing creatures and all have the free will to make our own choices. Don't let books and descriptions weigh you down. Be who you want to be."

"Wow, those are powerfully inspiring words there." Alison declared with a smirk.

Horace shook his head, scraping the mud out of the horse's hooves. "You sure know how to deflate a balloon don't you."

Alison laughed, bumping him with her shoulder. "I'm just kidding. I know what you are saying. I guess at some point I need to come to terms with the fact that my heritage doesn't define me. My title doesn't define me, it's me that does."

"Yep, like me and my wild red hair. I embraced it, but you won't find the crazy in this boy, not unless you have some whiskey and a Texas football game."

Alison laughed shaking her head. "Never drank whiskey..."

"I'd hope not."

"And only watched football a couple of times. Humans are interesting with their contact sports."

"I heard that Tom Brady is an elf. Not really fair but he swears he never uses magic."

"Yeah." Alison scoffed. "Me either. Izzie told me about that story you were telling her."

"Yeah? Which one…"

"Mmhm." Alison got up from her stool and paced back and forth. "About the boy who killed someone with magic. If this kid had a following, was dabbling in dark magic, and ended up killing someone, even by accident, how did they let him go with no punishment?"

"Well, that's the next part of the story. When he went up in front of the Silver Griffins to tell them about what happened, he could see they already had their eye on him. The Silver Griffins, at the time, were in charge of handing down school punishments for the worst crimes. They started to question him on his dealings with dark magic, his collection of followers, and how he could have saved the boy if he really wanted to. They hounded this kid over and over, beating him up, pushing him around, until finally he snapped. He screamed to the council, telling them he wasn't sorry he died, it made him a better wizard. That he learned from his death, and that he would never again taste the strangling wrath of light magic."

"Wow."

"Uh, yeah." Horace chuckled, scooting his stool down to the back of the horse and picking up his back leg. "So, the council lost it and they expelled him from the school. He was underage so all they could do was remand him to the custody of someone on the council until his 18th birthday. Well, before they could come to collect him he disappeared and hid out until he came of age. No one had a clue where he went, they searched and searched but couldn't find him. Some think he created a portal back to Oriceran, but back then portals were highly regulated and there was no record of anything like that. Anyway, when he returned it was obvious that he had no remorse for his crimes. He was even darker than before, but because his talents were only so-so, the council just let him live, keeping an eye on him until they no longer feared him for a movement."

"So, what does he do now?"

"I don't know, probably has some gang or something. Works in the dark part of some Kemana. I really don't know."

"What was his name?"

"Andrew Parker. I'll remember that for the rest of my life. He used to scream at students who bullied him, 'I'm Andrew Parker and you're gonna pay.' It was my first year here at the school. To think I actually felt bad for the kid too."

"Man, that sucks, and to live with the fact that he killed his best friend. That had to have pushed him even further over the edge."

"Probably why he never tried to pick himself up again. Death does something to people."

Alison looked up at the horse, her mother flashing through her head. She knew that sentiment all too well. Death *definitely* did something to people, it made them fear, it made them mourn, and it made them stop living their lives to a certain degree, just because it felt like they couldn't take another step without breaking. Alison had been through all of that, and sometimes still felt it. She didn't want to talk about it though, she wasn't ready to open up like that, even to Horace.

The stables were quiet for a few moments, Alison was lost in her thoughts, and Horace gave her the space to do so. He finished up cleaning the horse's hooves then put up his stuff. He picked up his thick green coat and pulled it on, pulling a pair of fingerless gloves out of the pockets.

"Hey, you want to see something cool?"

"Sure." Alison was glad for the change of subject, she didn't want to ruin her night by dwelling so heavily on the past.

"Awesome, follow me. I would put those gloves on if I were you. One I can spot you in the dark, and two, it's a bit of a walk."

"Ha-ha…" Alison smirked and kicked Horace as he hurried past her with a smile.

She pulled on her warm gloves and wrapped her scarf tightly around her neck and over her mouth. The cold wind whipped through the barn as he pushed open the doors. Alison shoved her hands into her pockets and walked out, following him toward the tree line. They walked quickly next to the entrance of the forest as the dogs ran back and forth to stay warm. Their breath rose like clouds into the air and Alison half expected it to start snowing, though it was a little early for that.

They walked down the hill and crossed the valley then climbed another larger hill, and Horace helped her up the steep incline at the top. Once they were there, Horace stuck his arms out in front of him. It was pitch black, but Horace pulled out a lantern and lit it, casting light out ahead to guide his way. A smile moved across Alison's lips as she stared down at the energy coming up from a Christmas tree farm. Hundreds of perfectly cropped trees grew below them, some small but most mature.

"How long have you been growing these?"

"Well, I do them in two batches. The smaller ones are a year old and the bigger ones are two years old."

"I didn't know they grew that fast."

"They don't, but that's the glory of having a school full of magical folks." Horace gave her a huge grin.

"What are you going to do with them?"

"They are for the Christmas decorations. This is a big place, so I'll be cutting them down and placing them all over."

"I see fairy souls down there."

"Yep, they take care of the trees for me until the season comes. It's a little cold for them but they love the holiday, so they do it for me."

"You have a serious way with magical creatures." Alison chuckled. "That's so cool. I can't wait to see them all up and decorated."

Horace pulled his coat together and shivered, looking up at the sky. "From the way the weather has been blowin' in, I'm thinking we just might have a white one this year, or at least a white one for the party. Everybody will be gone on Christmas."

"What about you? Are you going back to Austin?"

"Aunt Estelle wanted me to but I'm gonna stay here this year and take care of everything. I won't be alone, though. Some of the teachers stay here and have a good ole Christmas Eve Feast that I don't have to work for."

"That sounds fun."

"How about you?"

"Uh, I'm actually not sure. I know Brownstone and Shay are gonna come get me, so I guess we'll do whatever their normal is in California. Probably won't be a white Christmas there."

"Well, whatever you do, try to relax and have fun. You deserve it."

"Thanks, Horace. And thanks for growing all these trees! This is going to be amazing."

A light snow began to fall and Alison put out her hand feeling the cold, wet snowflakes hit her skin. The dogs sniffed where they fell, snorting into the cold grasses at her feet. Alison was happy that she would get to see how the energy of the mansion looked at Christmas. It made her warm inside, even standing there in the frost of the night.

Between the midterms, the night walks, and the celebrations, the weeks flew by for Izzie. She had learned to take better care of herself, making sure to get her *rest* in at least once a day. Taking a test exhausted was not how she wanted to end the first half of her high school career. When the last final was complete she walked out of the classroom, laughing at the students running up and down the halls. Everyone wore some sort of ugly Christmas sweater. She glanced at Scarlett, who was standing to the side with her crew. She gave Alison a daunting stare and whipped around, her red-and-green-dyed ponytail swirling behind her.

"Hey." Peter came running up beside her. Today's burn mark was on his pocket.

"Hey! I see you are getting better with your spells. Only a pocket this time."

"Yeah." He laughed, running a hand through his messy

hair. "You're coming to the Christmas Extravaganza Dinner thing tonight, right?"

"Isn't it mandatory?"

"No." Peter laughed. "Not by Berens, but in our crew of friends I'd say it's mandatory."

"Yes, then." She smiled. "I will be there with no bells on. Maybe a Christmas sweater, but no bells."

"That'll do." He looked over the heads of the other kids and saw Ethan waiting by the stairs. "Okay, I'll see you tonight!"

"Bye." she chuckled watching him trip over his feet and almost plow down a group of kids.

Alison made her way to the library. When she opened the doors, Leo was standing at the desk, dusting off a book. He didn't even look up, just yelled.

"No need to be in the library. Go home and eat a turkey, or whatever humans do."

"That's Thanksgiving." Alison smiled as Leo turned around. "I brought you a little gift to thank you for letting me use your books in Braille."

Alison handed him a wrapped rectangular gift, complete with a green bow. His expression softened for the first time since she had met him, and he looked up at her and back at the package. He unwrapped the gift carefully, acting as if it were the first present he had ever received. Who knew, maybe it was. When he pulled the paper off he smiled slightly.

Alison smiled back. "It was my favorite book as a kid.

Thought you might want to read something a magical being wrote here on Earth."

"*The Old Man and the Sea* by Ernest Hemingway," he read aloud. "I liked that Hemingway character. I was sad when he went back to Oriceran to live out his days. Thank you, Alison. It's very generous."

He bowed his head, holding onto his hat, and the flower bowed slightly as well. Alison bowed back and walked toward the door.

"And Alison?"

"Yes?" She looked over her shoulder. "Have a Merry Christmas."

"You too, sir."

Alison went back to the stairs, feeling good about the gifts she'd found for her friends, including the librarian. She had been able to go to the human town to pick up some things, and the rest were the trinkets she had purchased in the city underground. She headed next to the dorm room, where she found the girls chatting excitedly. Aya and Emma were finishing up their packing since they were leaving the next day. Kathleen had already finished.

"I can't wait to go to the islands for Christmas. I can work on my tan, drink coconut water on the beach, and just relax."

"My mom always bakes a ham, but she still hasn't gotten it quite right." Emma wrinkled her nose. "Last year she tried magic, and every time we cut into it, the thing snorted like a pig. We ended up giving it a proper burial and had frozen pizza and fruit snacks—but she put them on nice dishes."

Everyone laughed—even Emma, who knew she just

might be having the same feast that year as well. Aya moved her dolls across the room and carefully arranged them in her suitcase.

"My family does a turkey and a ham and all the normal human sides. They are waiting to decorate the tree until I get there, and they even invited Henry this year."

Alison smiled sweetly. "That sounds really nice."

Kathleen looked at Izzie, who was sitting on the edge of the bed. "How about you, Izzie?"

Izzie glanced at Alison, who gave her an encouraging look. She took a deep breath and let it out. "I grew up in an orphanage, so we really didn't do anything like that." Everyone stopped and looked at her, listening intently. "This year I am spending the holiday with Ms. Berens and her family since she is now my guardian. I'm sorry I didn't tell you guys before."

Kathleen put down the sweater she was holding and went to Izzie, leaning down and hugging her tightly. Izzie's eyes went wide and she slowly hugged her back, not having expected that at all. The girls started laughing at Izzie's reaction but Kathleen ignored them.

"Maybe next year you can come with me and *my* family."

"Thanks." Izzie smiled and glanced at Alison again, who shrugged.

Kathleen went back over to her bed and smiled. "Don't you love the holidays? They make everyone so kind and giving."

Emma smiled. "I think Kathleen drank the punch."

Kathleen grinned and waved her hands at Emma, pulling a white cashmere sweater over her satin tank top.

She looked in the mirror, fluffing her hair and making sure her jeans were tucked perfectly into her white-furred boots, then fixed her eyeliner.

"What are you wearing to the dinner, Alison?"

Alison held up her white hoodie, jeans, and tennis shoes. "This, I suppose. I don't really have a lot to choose from, and everything else is packed."

Kathleen sighed, swiping her finger across the edge of her lip. "I was going to wait until we were all exchanging gifts, but here." She laid a red bag in Alison's lap. "I think you need this now."

Alison grinned in delight and pulled out the sparkling tissue. In the bag was a soft light blue cashmere sweater. She held it out in front of her where Kathleen could see the thin strands of silver reflected against her white hair.

Alison hugged Kathleen. "Thank you! It's so soft, and it's one of the nicest thing I've ever owned."

"You are more than welcome," she replied. "Okay, who is ready to go?"

Emma shut her suitcase and nodded, glancing at her green sweater and winter white dress pants in the mirror. Aya stuck her hand in the air. Her cardigan was buttoned down the front, meeting her little flowing black and pink skirt perfectly. Alison quickly changed into her sweater and grabbed her bags of gifts from beside the bed. Kathleen led the troops out of the dorm, but Alison paused and grabbed Izzie's hand, dragging her groaning after them. She might not be able to fix whatever was wrong with Izzie, but she was going to make sure she had a good time at dinner.

As they entered the hall Alison's eyes lit up. There was

so much energy in the room! Izzie peeked around Alison and tried to fight back a smile, but she just couldn't. The tables had been moved, leaving an open space in the front in case anyone wanted to dance. Over a dance floor that resembled an ice-skating rink, magical snow fell from the ceiling, disappearing just at head-height. Lining the room were beautiful fresh Christmas trees that had been decorated with handmade magical ornaments that danced to the music. Their lights sparkled and shimmered, and each had a single candle on the very top that flickered in the dim light of the dining hall.

The tables had beautiful holiday centerpieces and bore traditional Earth Christmas foods. There was a ham, cranberry salad, green bean casserole, stuffing, mashed potatoes, sweet potatoes, and croissants stacked higher than the ham. Peter and Ethan were already at the table, but to the girls' surprise, they hadn't touched the food yet. Peter was wearing a pair of jeans with red suspenders and a green button-up shirt. Ethan was wearing his norm, only in his pocket was a red and green flower. The girls approached the table and took a seat, looking around as everyone talked excitedly and exchanged gifts.

"We should exchange gifts first," Kathleen pronounced.

"Can I go first?" Ethan pulled out six wrapped gifts that were all about the same size. He passed them around the table and watched as everyone opened theirs. Emma smiled at the carved piece of wood with her name perfectly etched into it, as well as a pair of otters underneath.

Each person got one, personalized as Ethan saw them. When Alison ran her fingers over hers there was no magic, and she realized that Ethan had carved them with his own two hands. These were what he had been working on the entire first half of the year. She could feel her name in the wood and two beautiful roses carved at the edges.

"Thank you, Ethan! This is an amazingly thoughtful gift."

Izzie held hers close to her chest. "It really is. I've never gotten anything like it."

Luke walked up to the table and smiled. Ethan pulled out another gift and handed it to him.

"Have a seat with us, buddy."

A chair appeared next to Alison, and he sat down and gave her a crooked smile. He opened his gift from Ethan, a hand-carved wolf, and nodded. "This is amazing! Thank you, man."

Kathleen pulled her bag into her lap. "Okay, okay, my turn. And Alison is wearing hers."

Alison smiled as Kathleen handed out gifts, even one to Luke. They were all specific to the person and all, not surprisingly, were clothes. Everyone was gracious, no one wanting to take away the excitement on Kathleen's face. Even Ethan hugged her, looking sideways at the bow tie with skulls on it she had gotten him.

Emma pulled out a stack of photo albums and handed them around the table.

"I took some after-school lessons with Mrs. Fowler, and she showed me how to create photo albums with the pictures I had stored in my memories. I hope you like them."

Izzie opened hers and looked down at the pictures, smiling widely. Emma had captured every happy moment she'd had since she had gotten to the school. She hadn't even realized how many happy moments there had been, and all because of the people at that table. It was such a thoughtful and meaningful gift. When she flipped to the back page she looked around, finding everyone with the same picture. It was the seven of them, standing in front of the school, their arms around each other. They were smiling and laughing together.

"How did you get a memory with you in it?"

"I didn't. I got it from one of the upperclassmen I remembered seeing there."

Izzie pulled out a satchel and dumped the contents on the table. They were all necklaces made from coins from Ruby Falls. She had used her magic to bend them into different shapes. She passed each one to its recipient and smiled happily as they all put them around their necks, even Kathleen. Alison held her hand over hers and felt the energy in it soothe her nerves. She leaned forward and kissed Izzie on the cheek.

"Thank you. It's wonderful."

Aya went next, handing out stories she had written throughout the year. Each one of them was a reflection of how she felt about her friends, and each had a stone from the underground city pressed into its leather-bound cover.

"It's the same story but told through my eyes and how I saw each of you."

Kathleen teared up, pressing her hand to her mouth and taking a deep breath. "That is so cool, Aya. Thank you."

"You're welcome. You're *all* welcome."

Peter cleared his throat and lifted a half-burnt bag to his lap.

"So, I tried to make each of you a trinket with that book

of old spells that I bought, but something went wrong. They all turned out fantastic, but halfway here the bag caught on fire. So, um…sorry."

The whole table burst into laughter. Peter chuckled, shrugged, and stuck the bag back under his chair. Ethan slapped him on the back.

"It's the thought that counts, brother."

Peter smiled and looked at Luke, who pulled out a small pouch from his pocket and set down seven round stone pieces. He cleared his throat and looked at the group.

"I told my father what you did during the fight in the city, and he sent these to me for you. They are our family shifter crest, dating back to Oriceran. There is one for each of you, and it signifies that you are part of our clan—for life. If there is ever anything you need, like help or anything, you can show any shifter this and they will stand for our family."

Alison smiled as he handed one to her. She ran her finger over the crest burned into the stone and put it into her pocket, then lifted a brown gift bag onto the table and looked at the others.

"I guess it's my turn then."

She pulled a long velvet box from the bag and handed it to Aya.

"I paid one of the upperclassmen to get this for you. I know you wanted it for your mom."

Aya opened the box and started to cry, then got up and hugged Alison tightly.

"That is the best gift you could have given me. She will love it. Thank you."

Alison pulled the next four pieces from her bag and handed them to Kathleen, Ethan, Emma, and Peter.

"Those are trinkets you can put on your necklaces or keep in your pocket. Kathleen, yours is for beauty; it will keep you forever young. Ethan, yours is for bravery, Peter, curiosity, and Emma's is for kindness."

"Thank you." Emma smiled.

Alison handed Izzie a small box, and she pulled out a long silver chain with a star pendant. She looked at Alison with curiosity.

"My mother always told me that no matter how far apart we were, when we looked at the sky we would see the same stars. I have one that matches yours."

Alison pulled the star from under her sweater and smiled. Izzie nodded and smiled back, putting hers on and holding the star in her palm. Alison pulled the last gift out handing it to Luke and he unwrapped it to find a leather-bound journal.

"That journal is magic. Anytime you feel angry or upset because people tell you that you don't belong, write about it in that journal. It will write back to you with comforting words."

"That's so cool! Thank you."

Everyone exchanged hugs and settled down in their chairs, then Ethan stretched and announced, "Well, enough of this sappy shit, let's eat!"

The whole table laughed and began to talk excitedly, spending their first Christmas dinner together in their new home away from home.

29

It was finally the last day of school and the mansion was abuzz with students greeting their parents. They were all leaving for Christmas break—all except Izzie, who wasn't exactly sure what was happening. She just knew she would be with Ms. Berens. Kathleen, Emma, and Aya had already gone downstairs with their luggage to wait for their parents. Alison folded up her sweater from the night before and put it in her suitcase. Izzie stood at the foot of her bed looking at the empty closet.

Alison locked up her suitcase, making sure to carefully set it on the floor. The egg was wrapped up inside. She really didn't want to take it with her, but she didn't know where else to put it while she was gone. She went to Izzie and put her hands on her shoulders.

"You'll be fine. You get to spend the holiday with a real family, though I'm not sure what you should expect."

Izzie displayed her best smile and nodded. "I'm sure it will be fine. And it's only for a couple of weeks, anyway."

"That's right. Before you know it, you will be back on that bed rolling your eyes at Kathleen and watching Aya move dolls with her mind."

Izzie laughed and grasped her star pendant. "Thanks for being such a good friend."

"Thank you, too. Now, come downstairs and meet the mess I will be spending the holiday with." Alison smiled and picked up her suitcase, draping her coat and scarf over it.

The two girls made their way through the crowds of parents and students. When they reached the bottom of the steps Kathleen ran over, throwing her arms around both of them.

"My parents are ready to go, but I couldn't leave without saying goodbye."

Izzie grunted as she tried to catch her breath. "Have fun in the islands."

Kathleen pulled back, grinning. "Thanks. I'll bring you back a tiki statue."

Alison pulled her eyebrows together, slightly confused and Kathleen bounced away as her parents waved goodbye to the two of them. Izzie sighed and went over to Ms. Berens. Alison followed close behind, setting her suitcase carefully on the floor.

The headmistress turned to Alison. "You have done wonderfully this semester, minus the mishap in the city. I hope you have a wonderful Christmas, Alison. I'll take good care of Izzie."

"Thank you, Ms. Berens. You have a good holiday as well."

Just then the front doors blew open and white powdery

snow blew across the floor of the foyer. Brownstone and Shay rushed in, closing the doors quickly behind them and ignoring the people staring at them. Alison chuckled and shook her head as they scanned the room. Brownstone looked ready for a mission in his tight brown shirt, brown leather jacket, and army fatigue pants with boots. Shay was dressed similarly, only instead of her usual tight tank top she was wearing a black high-neck fleece sweater with a Christmas-tree pin on the shoulder.

Izzie leaned over to Alison. "Can I assume they are with you?"

"Yep." Alison laughed.

"Hey, kiddo," Brownstone said, patting her on the shoulder.

Shay wrapped her arms around Alison and squeezed, her pin poking into Alison's skin. "How are you? You look fantastic. Do you like my pin? I'm trying to fit in here."

"Very festive." Alison chuckled. "And we are a group of misfit toys, so I think you will be just fine."

"Shay, James, this is Izzie. She's like my best friend here." Brownstone and Shay shook her hand, although the bounty hunter eyed the Light Elf suspiciously.

Izzie and Ms. Berens had to talk to some other people, so Alison took Shay and James through the classrooms, explaining what she had learned so far. She stopped and showed them the list of grades posted at the top of the stairs and Brownstone gloated at all the A's next to Alison's name.

When they were about ready to leave, Brownstone and Shay shook their heads and looked at each other. Alison had seen that look before, and she knew there was something they needed to tell her, so she pulled them into the dining hall and shut the doors behind them. The place was empty, since breakfast was over and everyone was leaving for the day. A plate appeared on the table where her hand was, but she waved it away.

"No food, thank you." She turned back to Shay and Brownstone. "Okay, what's up? I can see it."

Brownstone cleared his throat. "The Harriken are still active."

Alison stumbled back from them and looked around the room. The Harriken were the Asian Gang that had killed her mother, but the last she had heard before she left for school they were no longer active. Fear blew through her every time she heard their name. All she could see was her mother's face, and all she could feel was the anger boiling over. She couldn't let it get to her, though. She had come too far. The first half of the school year had changed the way she saw things and going back would be a mistake. She took in a deep breath and shut her eyes, remembering the bravery she'd displayed in the underground city. She turned back to Shay and Brownstone and nodded.

"Okay, what does that mean for me?"

"Nothing really," Brownstone replied. "Just that we will have to head somewhere that isn't LA, at least for this holiday."

Shay elbowed Brownstone in the side and forced a smile at Alison. "Of course, we will figure out a way to make it like Christmas. Right, Brownstone?"

"Oh, yes," he agreed with a blank look on his face.

Alison knew neither one of them had any idea what to do for Christmas. They had no experience with it, and from the look of Shay's pin, she was trying to get an idea from department stores. Alison lifted an eyebrow as they stared at each other.

"We can hang that green stuff wherever we go." Shay pointed her finger. "And decorate a tree."

"Oh, yeah." Brownstone nodded. "There are trees everywhere."

Alison tried to hold back a giggle.

"And we can have a Christmas pizza for dinner." Shay nodded astutely.

"Or maybe Christmas barbeque." Brownstone sounded completely out of his element.

Alison sighed and turned toward the doors. "Come on, guys, we'll figure it out as we go."

Back in the entry hall Alison wrapped her arms gently around Izzie, who had come back to see her off, and gave her a squeeze. She whispered in her ear, "You are going to be fine. By the looks of it, *I'm* the one who's gonna be eating Christmas barbeque and decorating a redwood."

Izzie pulled back, confused. Alison shook her head and rolled her eyes. "Don't ask."

Izzie giggled and nodded. "I think someone else wants to say goodbye."

Alison followed Izzie's stare over to the corner where Horace was standing, wearing a Santa Hat and smiling. Alison laughed and nodded at Izzie before grabbing her bright orange scarf off her suitcase. She went to Horace and looked around at all the decorations, leaning forward and looking out at the lawn. Christmas trees lined the drive, the lights glimmering against the deep white powdery snow.

"You got your white Christmas."

Horace nodded. "I sure did. Are those your people?"

Alison looked over her shoulder at Shay and Brownstone, who were standing awkwardly next to her suitcase. "Yes, I suppose they *are* my people."

Horace nodded with a smile. "We can't always pick our family."

"Very true." Alison lifted the scarf and draped it around Horace's neck. "And you, sir, need to stay warm while I am gone. This is not Austin, Texas. And thank the fairies for me. The trees are amazing."

"I will." Horace glanced at Ms. Berens who nodded to him. He pulled a small yellow stone from his pocket and reached out, putting it in Alison's palm. "If you need anything while you are gone, just hold this stone and send your energy through it. We will get the signal. Okay? Not just for this holiday, but anytime you are away."

Alison looked down at the stone and nodded, putting it into her pocket. She leaned forward and gave Horace a hug. "I'll miss you. Take those walks without me."

"Yeah right." he laughed. "No students mean long nights of sleep."

Alison laughed. "I'll see you in a couple of weeks. Merry Christmas."

"Merry Christmas."

Alison went to Shay and Brownstone and picked up her suitcase, careful of the egg inside. She looked back at Izzie and smiled. The cold air hit her as Brownstone opened the front door and she stepped out into the snow.

At the car, Brownstone took her suitcase with a grunt and carefully put it into the trunk. She looked out over the hills and pastures, seeing the souls of the small magical beings celebrating in their own way. The energy of the fairies danced through the leaves of the trees, giving Alison her own little light show.

Shay walked up beside her and looked out at the forest, unable to see the energy streams. "Whatcha looking at?"

"Nothing." Alison smiled. "Let's go get some Christmas pizza."

FINIS

Alison's powers continue to grow. Good thing because the dark wizarding families are planning something wicked...

Alison's story continues in <u>BRIGHT IS HER SIGHT</u>.

Solve a murder, save her mother, and stop the apocalypse?

No problem!

She has a foul-mouthed troll on her side.

Magic is real, and it's coming back with a literal bang.

AVAILABLE ON AMAZON RETAILERS AND IN
KINDLE UNLIMITED

Will the *real* Judith Berens please stand up?

Okay, that's myself and Michael Anderle. We wanted to give everyone a break from seeing our names splashed across a cover – do a little homage to the Berens women of Oriceran and a nod to the wonderful, Judith Anderle (Michael's stupendous other half).

I'm six weeks away (give or take) from moving into my new home that Oriceran built and is way beyond where I ever hoped to get to in this lifetime. It's not a mansion as mansions go – but it is to me.

Got me thinking about 2008 and the Great Recession when I had everything in storage at one point and was living in a hotel while I followed around a former South African Navy Diver and diamond mine owner to write his life story. I had just gone skydiving for the first time, accompanying him on one of his favorite pastimes and was back at the hotel.

I was in the elevator and had the hotel key and the

rental car key in my hand and that was it. No fixed address. Felt kind of liberating, mostly because I knew this was just a moment in time. Looking back, it's remarkable that I didn't catastrophize into the future wondering how I'd crawl back to having a household. Wasn't worried.

Some of that may come from growing up poor and making a dollar stretch in remarkable ways. The rest of it was a choice to just not worry and enjoy the present moment. I think right before that job I was hired to work on a book about the most possessed house in America, according to the American Catholic Church. (It's in Pittsburgh). One of their leading exorcists did a prayer of protection over me for 30 minutes before I was allowed to go into the house and even then I was warned – it might not be enough.

Money might have been short, but adventure was always there.

Reminds me of a story my late father told me about growing up in Richmond, Virginia during the Great Depression. He delivered newspapers in the afternoon to the tent city that had sprung up along Cary Street filled with formerly middle class families who were reduced to nothing. (Yes, papers were considered a necessity and families would buy one together… different times) Some of the time he was expected at cotillion right after he was done pitching papers. He didn't have much either, but they were an old Virginia family and he was still expected to attend cotillion. (Precursor to debutante falderol senior year of high school). He'd ride his bike through the tent city in his hand-me-down tux, throwing papers to families worried about food and shelter. His mother, my grandmother, took in boarders to make ends meet.

His daughter, her granddaughter will soon be standing in a very nice, new house with a lot of nice touches – all because of a swearing troll and a magical Jasper elf – and now a regular cast of characters – and Michael Anderle. My dreams, hard work and a lot of great fans got me here.

Way back then as my dad pedaled his bike… or my grandmother took in boarders… and years ago when I stood there holding only those two keys… there was no way to know what twists and turns the story was going to take. Imagine if any of us had given up because it didn't look the way we imagined in that moment. So many great adventures – so many more to come. Thank you everyone!

AUTHOR NOTES - MICHAEL ANDERLE

WRITTEN JUNE 2, 2018

First, THANK YOU for not only reading this story, but reading our author notes as well! If this is the first book of mine you've read, an ADDITIONAL thank you for trying us out!

Alison is a special girl in my life. She is the young woman that broke into my life over a year ago and would forever change multiple lives.

She is, in fact, the one who was the catalyst for what became the Oriceran Universe.

You see, I have another series called The Unbelievable Mr. Brownstone (for those that don't know) and it was Alison that took him out of his comfortable life catching bounties and propelled him into existence.

It was the short, short story of Alison meeting James Brownstone that was the impetus for me talking with Martha Carr about writing a series (which became a Universe) together.

Dozens of books later, we are releasing the book about the young woman that cared for a scared dog and made a fateful call to his owner.

From that phone call came collaborations with many wonderful and talented authors including: Martha Carr, Sarah Noffke, Abby Lynn Knorr, SM (Sarah) Boyce, Flint Maxwell and others.

I hope you have fallen for Alison as I have.

Drizzt

My first experience with a Drow hero is Drizzt Do'Urdin in The Icewind Dale trilogy published between 1988 and 1990. Ever since then, I've LOVED the idea of a Drow hero, yet I've never had a reason to write one.

Until Alison.

The relationship between Alison and James Brownstone cannot be more convoluted if one tried (and I did). However, it could not be more normal and loving with how much they care about each other. Along with Shay, they are going to be one family that can rock the world(s) and the world in between for those who need them, and for each other if they can get over their own issues.

Don't make her angry

For those who would think the blind girl is a push-over, I suggest you don't make her angry.

You won't like it very much if Alison gets angry.

I'd say her dark side might come out, but I'll just change that to say *her Drow side might show...*

See you next book!

Ad Aeternitatem,
  Michael Anderle

OTHER REVELATION OF ORICERAN
UNIVERSE BOOKS

SCHOOL OF NECESSARY MAGIC

SCHOOL OF NECESSARY MAGIC: RAINE CAMPBELL

ALISON BROWNSTONE

THE DANIEL CODEX SERIES

THE LEIRA CHRONICLES

I FEAR NO EVIL

THE UNBELIEVABLE MR. BROWNSTONE

REWRITING JUSTICE

THE KACY CHRONICLES

MIDWEST MAGIC CHRONICLES

SOUL STONE MAGE

THE FAIRHAVEN CHRONICLES

**JOIN THE ORICERAN UNIVERSE FAN GROUP ON
FACEBOOK!**

Martha Carr Social

Website: http://www.marthacarr.com

Facebook:
https://www.facebook.com/groups/MarthaCarrFans/

Michael Anderle Social

Website: http://kurtherianbooks.com/

Email List: http://kurtherianbooks.com/email-list/

Facebook Here:
https://www.facebook.com/TheKurtherianGambitBooks/